MW00910556

# When Hannah Met

# Charlie

# Table of contents

From the blog:

13. We feel eager before we feel ready

14. We feel patient when time is our only hope

15. We feel in control until we've rescinded all rationale

16. We feel comfortable until we see the light

## Offline:

1. We feel a void when drained of desire

2. We feel doubtful of the past while stuck in the present

3. Untitled

4. We feel insecure without shame

5. We feel angry when others go unscathed

6. We take what we can get when there isn't much for getting

7. We feel jealous when there's nothing for holding onto

8. We can compromise until we're at the end of the line

9. We live in memories because we're lost in the now

10. We feel guarded until no one's interested

11. We call it love because we don't know its name

12. We feel guilty when there's nothing to be done

13. We feel determined despite the walls between us

14. We feel love with contact until contact defines our love

15. The Secret Garden

# From the blog

# The flower that failed to love

Dedicated to Zachary Parker

Charlie loved the way that Hannah smelled. Once he got a whiff of her, he could not resist inhaling her scent at every opportunity he got.

And really, his opportunities were endless. It came down to a matter of willpower. The chance to rush through Hannah's delicate petals and sweep up her smell was always available; if only constant wind were not so unhealthy. Charlie was the breeze, he was the movement of little particles of air, the dance of shifting pressures in the atmosphere.

If he wanted he could spend his days endlessly rushing Hannah. But wants could not be as great as needs, and he needed to resist for the sake of Hannah. Constant abrasion by the wind would eventually wear her down, rip away her petals altogether, leave her wilting and worn. It was a delicate balance of desire and restraint. She was worth it, though, he realized because as he initially loved her smell, he grew to love the flower entirely more than he ever imagined was possible.

What was it about Hannah's smell in particular that had started it all off, though? Why couldn't he just breeze across every field of flowers and find contentedness in the aroma? Well, because each flower has their own unique scent, and Hannah's happened to be exquisite, the most delicious of all of the flowers as far as Charlie was concerned. She was the only one for him.

Others sensed the splendor of Hannah's smell as well. The other flowers, on a regular basis, insisted that her fragrance was irresistible. Hannah could hear them and she could smell the things that they were saying, but something deeply ingrained within her caused her to sway in the breeze always in disbelief.

It was cliché and stupid, for a blooming flower to see herself only as flawed, but that did not prevent it from ruining what she and Charlie had slowly begun to have.

It was a sort of cognitive dissonance, an internal conflict, when she was piled high with these compliments, yet none around her swayed in her direction or seemed to really love her. They insisted that she smelled great, but was there anything else great about Hannah?

At least Charlie did not insist that she smelled lovely. It was obvious in his actions, though, and that was enough to leave Hannah feeling stricken. She noticed as his resistance waned and waned, the days grew windier and windier, and her self-regard slithered away through her roots and into the desolate soil which she'd known for her whole life.

A part of her basked in it, and sometimes her petals opened wider, spreading and soaking in the love. Her hue grew brighter, and her scent only stronger. Charlie was the best at dancing, lead her just so, and he brought warm air when Hannah felt uneasily cool and refreshing breezes when the sun sweltered. Her love for him only grew and grew with each passing day.

Somehow, still, love inspired self-hatred in Hannah.

The love for something as insignificant about her as her scent left her devastated about her character as an actual flower. She questioned her petals, her stem, her stamens, her leaves, the way she must have felt as he curved along her body, anything that Charlie might see as flawed. It was the issue that the praise caused her to doubt, doubt the sincerity, and the integrity of her entire being. Hannah began to hate herself as the love piled on.

As a budding flower, still developing her scent producing glands, she had never thought that she might detest, grow sickened by, the constant insistence that her perfume was beautiful. But one fateful day, it did. She could not take it anymore. The insistence was too much and it all just felt so fake and degrading to the rest of her, and it hurt.

When Charlie eased his way onto her field that afternoon and gently brushed past her, Hannah inhaled sharply, sucking her petals together only to close herself off from the outside world. It was as if she was back to being a bud.

At first, Charlie realized that she needed space. The days were calm for a while; no kites were flown. After a week though, a week of waiting for Hannah to blossom open and release her aroma to the sky, he began to grow impatient. Though he did not really mean to, he picked up much too strongly. He began to jostle her, blow too hard, and thrash her around.

It was only because he loved her so much.

A part of her understood, and a part of her almost opened back up to Charlie. After all, she loved the way he made her feel when she got out of her own head. It was only when she was lost in her flower thoughts that Charlie's adoration made her hate herself. So, she could push away her own mind, let herself fall into things and feel like she might be in love again. But it did not feel true to herself. At that point she may as well be uprooted, she figured, swept up into the sky with him. There, she could love him infinitely, but what was the point if she could not love herself?

The sky was not where she belonged, and so Hannah held on, stayed closed, and continued to flop in the wind.

Until one day she flopped too hard. The weight of her top caused the plant to snap in a particularly strong gust. Right in the middle, she just tore, and cool, sticky liquid oozed from her wound.

Charlie ceased moving entirely, dumbfounded by what he had done. When he thought that all he'd done was love her, he did not realize he was killing her all along. The sky told him that he ought not to blame himself, that Hannah clearly had some issues of her own. She lay there bleeding, though, because of his actions no matter what anyone said.

Without their love, it was like all of the pressure in the air, in the entire atmosphere, zeroed out. He simply could not bring himself to blow. Not without the sweet scent of Hannah somewhere waiting.

More than that, though, he could not go on without her tender leaves and her gentle climb upward toward the sun, without her rich pink petals and most of all her deep love that she had felt for him in return, all of the things about her that truly made him love her so.

# The rock that remained

# dormant

Dedicated to Zachary Kanzler

Charlie had been smoothed and eroded for years and years in his home. That was really the only change he ever experienced. Otherwise, the days blended together in a perhaps boring but always peaceful way.

He enjoyed the forest, liked the darkness that eventually befell him when the canopy above grew thick enough. The ever changing seasons pleased him, kept things interesting and helped the time to pass. It was unfortunate, but Charlie had begun to exist only for the passage of time. This did not seem unfortunate to him until he met Hannah, though.

In the grand scheme of things, Hannah approached very quickly. One spring, a somewhat cooler spring than the average spring, she just seemed to sprout from the cracks and the ground surrounding him. She took her time in approaching

Charlie, at first merely creeping across the surface of the forest floor. In the beginning it was not clear that all of her circling and surrounding only had her headed in one direction: to his surface.

Hannah loved the forest as much as he did, appreciating the moisture around her that allowed any moss, but especially Hannah, to flourish. And boy did she love the view. Above her, incredible shadows covered her surroundings, shadows of pointy and rounded leaves alike creating impeccable patterns. She especially loved the view of Charlie, the boulder that had first caught her eye.

In retrospect, she would find it silly that she had entirely dictated her existence based on Charlie's presence. In the moment, though, as she slowly came to know him, it seemed like the best decision of her life. Charlie was gentle, but firm. And he had so much knowledge.

Hannah was impressed with the things he knew. It seemed as if he'd been in the forest forever, soaking in the goings on and pondering them, coming to incredible conclusions. Hannah herself was so preoccupied with growing that she missed quite a bit. In fact, it seemed the only goings on that did not pass her by were those which pertained to Charlie.

She knew when he shifted in the Earth, she knew when water had pooled along his surface, when animals had burrowed near him, and especially when other plants crossed his path. Sometimes it made her feel guilty in a sense, the depth with which she was involved with Charlie; that was, until she realized that he felt the same way.

The day that he invited her to his surface, Hannah exploded with growth. It was not necessarily that she grew outward; she was in no hurry to cover and overwhelm him with this love she'd been festering for months. She grew thicker, though, grew in on herself and became that much greener, that much more lush.

At first it was exactly what she expected, and that was everything she wanted. He simply smiled at her as she continued to grow, and they continued to become one big, green entity. The other rocks stared enviously and unadorned.

The other mosses continued to creep along trees and through the soil, but Hannah could feel their presence encroaching.

Because Hannah and Charlie appeared to have something perfect going. Never was a bitter word murmured; they never heated in anger, only in the sunlight; and their eternal closeness was envied by all. A moss had never hugged so closely to another surface as Hannah did to Charlie, and he held onto her too, his grainy surface like Velcro she could adhere to.

When it rained she melted into him. Yet his surface grew cold in the rain drops.

In the night, well they could no longer peer at one another. The darkness left them only tactile, so they felt each other, at first hesitantly, wondering if the other might mind, and then eagerly as the space between them seeped away. As Hannah somehow became even closer to Charlie, she began to wonder if he had looked on her the same way she had always seen him.

He had seen so much more than she had over the years, was so much more eternal. Could she mean the same thing to him as he meant to her?

Because he was her everything. And suddenly in the night it began to hurt as they pressed together and she wondered and wondered. Charlie was not prone to change the same way that Hannah was, and she began to voice her fears about it to him.

"Will you still love me if I'm dried up in a drought? Or if I simply lose the will to grow so bright green?"

"I'll always love you," he murmured in the stone voice that was always a bit too distant.

Hannah paid close attention. She realized that every kiss was a kiss that she initiated, every touch was a touch of her organic essence caressing his inorganic one. She withered in it, withered in jealousy that he could be so indifferent, so stone cold. Whereas she was swayed by every breeze, he remained still no matter what the weather, and he remained still no matter how much she proclaimed her love.

It was silly to question Charlie's behavior, it was simply the way he was. There was really nothing else that she could ask of him or expect of him. Perhaps if she had encroached upon a lake bed or on the bark of a living tree, then she could ask more of the love. But Charlie was stone, and there was simply nothing else he could offer.

Despite this knowledge, Hannah let her emotions get the best of her. For the first time, she burst out, spores surging from her every surface as she cried and begged of him why don't your actions reflect your words, how can you say that you love me while not showing your love for me at all?

Still, Charlie did not move.

At last Hannah came to the realization that her efforts were futile. Charlie would not change. If she wanted something else, well she would have to go after what she wanted. So, slowly at first and then quite quickly, she pulled off of his surface, detaching from the grainy parts and the smooth, slick surfaces of Charlie where water had bonded them, and at last she let go. A harsh wind swept her up, up and away from Charlie, one cool fall day.

The autumn sun was setting as Hannah too settled on the dark, earthy ground. Fallen leaves surrounded her and comforted her, but she did not need comfort, because after all, this was what she'd wanted. The wind could not carry her far enough away, though, and Hannah heard when he finally responded.

It was harsh, incredibly loud against the quiet forest. Charlie cracked, an earsplitting separation of his surface that started at his center and broke him in two.

Only then did Hannah cry, crying to know that only her absence, her negative actions, could illicit change. Not her love, but the revoking of her love, could bring him to at last show the love which he felt. But it was too late to go back, and so she sank into the forests' grass, and remained confident that this was better for the both of them because this was how they were supposed to love.

Not close, because their closeness was never enough, but far apart.

# The iceberg that could not stay afloat

Dedicated to Lance Johnson

Hannah was a sublime iceberg, an iceberg of massive proportions. She had all the right characteristics of ice, expanded as she froze from water and was able to buoy atop the sea. Hannah emerged from a crack far, far South along the polar ice cap, and she escaped from all of that frozen only to find herself completely immersed in Charlie.

Charlie caught her easily with his outstretched ocean arms, and held her tenderly as Hannah was slowly drawn away from the icecap that she had for so long called home.

He had had his eye on Hannah for a while, watching as he grew closer to her with each shifting tide. When she first noticed the way he lapped at her shores, she hesitated. But it did not take long for her to fall head over heels for Charlie.

The warmth of his waters against her iciness had a tendency to bite, but it was the good kind of bite, and his saltiness reminded her of tears of joy. Charlie's currents, she could tell even from afar, were gentle, but just strong enough to lead in some kind of dance if she ever got the chance. And his color, oh his color left her swooning. When all Hannah had ever known was white, was emptiness, or soft sky blue, it was inevitable that she fell deeply in love with Charlie's deep, mysterious, and vast dark blueness.

So when she began to creak and moan at the edges, she was excited to collapse into Charlie's awaiting tides. Neither of them at first let on to their excitement, or their anticipation at their at last being joined. At first, they both wore masks of vague interest, when, inside, they were bursting.

Charlie was excited to show Hannah his world. He swept her away, eager to introduce her to new forms of life which she had never imagined. The sea life left her frozen in amazement: fish with brilliant colors, and new breeds of penguins, even puffins with their round orange beaks. He showed her weather so unlike the icy snow she had known, rain droplets sizzling against her in a somewhat painful, but mostly exciting, way.

The way Charlie's intense blue hue had once impressed her so, Hannah loved the new colors. The sea floor was such a rich, healthful golden brown, and the plants that she came to see were an amazing shade, something so alien: green.

Unfortunately, there were unforeseen consequences to Hannah and Charlie's developing love.

Although he cared for her infinitely, he could not always help which ways his tides and currents pulled. And Hannah had really begun to stray from the deep south of the icecaps. Charlie loved her, but he could not protect her from the aspects of his existence which were out of his control. So, he watched in agony as Hannah began to shrink.

It was the blazing sun overhead, reaching more and more dangerous angles by the day, that did her in. The sun had no sympathy, no understanding for Hannah and Charlie's love. The sun only continued to seep energy into the atmosphere, in the deliberate form of heat which continued to diminish Hannah.

Charlie tried and tried to shield her, to draw her back to the South where she could be cool and safe and free to grow into an even more glorious iceberg. Hannah could not flourish with him, he began to realize. And while he had thought that his sweeping her up had been the best decision of his life, his greatest joy, it was becoming clear that this decision just might ruin her.

He told her, in a wave of frothy foam, frothy with his tears, that he had to return her to the place where they had first come together. He told her that it was not what he wanted, but what she needed if she were to survive. She told him that she valued their love more than anything, that she would not let go, not if the sun scorched her in one blazing burst of fury.

Hannah did not have much of a say, though, not while atop Charlie. So he began the journey slowly, hesitantly, even though he knew that he was only worsening his own pain by taking his time in letting go of their love. Still, he lurched on, growing colder by the moment.

That was when Hannah began to sink.

"I will not say goodbye," she creaked as the sunlight caused another giant crack along her surface. There was nothing Charlie could do as Hannah slipped below his surface, became a part of him forever, never to let go.

She sank all the way down to Charlie's floor, resting against the soft planes of his sand. As she lay there, perhaps dying, Charlie rushed tidal waves, tsunamis, against her, trying with all of his might to wrench her from the ocean floor. Hannah was determined, though. She loved him too much to let go.

As the seasons changed, the winds changed, the currents changed, and more warm water flooded through Charlie. It was only a matter of time before the water began to bite holes into Hannah's icy skin and course through her, wearing away at her. Hannah was not sad, though, not as she melted.

Because this meant that she would be with Charlie forever. Sure, he loved her glacial form, the smooth curves of her ice as it glistened in the sunlight, the way she floated, half amidst him half open to the sky, the noises that she made as he carried her along the coasts and her ever-changing structure creaked and moaned. He could love her this way, too, she explained, with her also being water and being integrated into every aspect of his existence.

They would become one, she insisted.

So Charlie let go, just let Hannah and the world around him take their courses. As soon as he gave in, well it seemed as if it were only moments before she melted.

Suddenly, though, Charlie realized that it was easy to surround her, embrace her from every side and hold her closer than ever before. And he realized that he could appreciate her curves as she, icy water, made contact and swirled amidst his own warm waters. He realized this was still his Hannah, the same Hannah he had made eyes at so long ago.

A wave of joy overcame him, and Hannah held on for dear life as they crashed into their love again at full force, this time bonded for an eternity.

# The little star that ran away

Dedicated to Kirstin Mattioli

Hannah had spent her entire existence expending energy. It was all she did and all she was meant to do. Her molten surface and fiery core were composed of reactions that had one sole purpose: creating energy for Hannah's little solar system.

And a lovely little solar system she had created. Six planets, all revolving around her, the products of her energy. Without Hannah, these planets and all of the elements on them, in them, would not exist or at least would not have direction. She gave them gravity.

Hannah regarded what she had made and what she had become as quite wonderful. Hannah's existence was colorful and brilliant, deep oranges flashing and yellow like egg yolks bursting along her surface. Her heat was like nothing else, she was sure; it blazed and turned the oceans of her planets to soft gases. Hannah was sure she was wonderful. That was, until she met Charlie.

Charlie was a star a few solar systems away. And Charlie shined so brightly. Hannah knew, from the moment she saw him, that she would love Charlie. Charlie was gentle, but he blazed hot; he was, as far as she was concerned, the perfect star.

For a while Hannah enjoyed the period before she and Charlie really loved each other. It was anxiety-ridden, though, and Hannah began to neglect her own solar system because she was so preoccupied with his. Anyway, compared to Charlie, everything about her seemed inadequate. It began to seem irrelevant, pointless as far as investing energy into it.

Hannah began to shine less brightly. Charlie, though, had enough light for the both of them and he somehow saw past Hannah's infinite flaws, the way her planets sometimes slipped out of their rotations and her fluctuating ability to give off energy. So Hannah and Charlie began to shine for one another, and she fell more deeply in love than she ever imagined was possible.

Hannah was so focused on Charlie and the love they shared, their shared luminescence, that she neglected her own existence entirely, and Hannah began to die. A dying star is a sad sight. Charlie did not seem to notice, though, as the fission reactions deep inside Hannah faded. Their shared light was so bright that he could not see as she began to go out.

In a way, Charlie was the worst thing to ever happen to Hannah.

The universe became chaotic, threw them curve balls like meteors and bending of the laws of physics. And one day Hannah noticed that she and Charlie were being pulled apart. That was the way the universe worked; she should have seen it coming. The universe was always expanding; it was inevitable that a gap between them would expand infinitely as well.

When Charlie told her that he could no longer see her, that her fading light had slipped from his line of sight, that he needed to let go of her to continue on his journey through empty space, Hannah was not really a star anymore. Whereas before Hannah had simply let go of herself, in this moment Hannah began to self-destruct, she turned on herself. Rather than passively let her solar system turn to ash and emptiness, she began to pursue such a change.

Things became infinitely cold quickly.

Charlie did not just let himself be pulled along either. He needed to leave Hannah behind, so he propelled himself out deeper into the universe. He was headed South while Hannah simply faded. Charlie blazed bright, as he slowly said "Goodbye," in an intimate solar flare. His heat touched her one last time.

Hannah could not say anything back; her ability to create light had been fatally compromised. And in turn, her ability to feed life was gone. It is unclear whether life ever existed in her solar system, hers or Charlie's, but if it was there, it was soon gone. Hannah became a dwarf star, red light casting an eerie glow over her planets' surfaces.

Every now and then, Charlie looked back, his white light blinding those in between the pair of distant stars. His light no longer reached Hannah, though; she couldn't even feel the heat of his pity or absence anymore.

The star that Hannah had been, she was long gone. In fact, the entire solar system had died. If Hannah waited much longer, she would burst, all of the energy lost in her dwarfing bursting forth and obliterating all that had once been.

The idea of shattering the traces of Charlie, if only in heat scars along her planets' surfaces and if only in light glimmers still reflecting off her moons, broke Hannah's little star heart.

So, there was only one solution. For her love to survive in any way, while still burning herself without bursting or shriveling to nothing, Hannah had to run away. She had become small, small enough to slip through the spaces in her solar system, in between all that existed there. She would sneak past the shadows of other, brilliant stars. Hannah would shoot to a corner of the universe where none would ever find her and where perhaps she could someday find the energy to burn blue again.

Charlie saw it out of the corner of his gravitational pull, deep in the blackness of the universe; he saw a brilliant spark of white trailing across the night sky. Part of him knew it was Hannah, but the majority of him could not accept this fact for the sake of his own happiness, his own ability to light the sky.

Hannah landed somewhere far away. She never exactly figured out where she was, she never exactly reached her full potential again. The reactions churning through her were never quite the same. So she made light and heat again, she turned back on like a slowly lifted dimmer. Hannah somehow remained a star. But she never stopped wondering if Charlie missed her heat, if her planets missed her heat: if anyone cared when she ran away.

# The sun that could no longer kiss

Dedicated to Darlene Kanzler

Charlie stared eastward every morning in anticipation, past the sandy shores, the dunes, and the soft whispering grasses. Hannah rose slowly, almost painfully slowly, every day. Each morning it was a little bit like seeing her for the first time again, her brilliant glow and perfect roundness. The smile that illuminated her face, and that then illuminated the sky, seemed to wake him up again.

She boiled him at the surface.

Hannah liked waking up to Charlie too. When they first met, were introduced as the Earth settled into its existence in her solar system, Charlie made her blush. She blazed warmer every morning as she moved westward across the sky, closer and closer to Charlie. The afternoons always heated slowly but intensely, and Charlie could perceive the change, felt as she tickled his waves with her rays.

He just loved the way that she'd always made him sparkle, lit him up, refracted light off of his every edge and made him better for it. They came to call it love at first sight as their relationship grew on and they continued to explain it, saw more and more the irresistibility of their attraction. There was no other explanation for the instant connection, the speed with which they grew close together at the horizon.

They kissed on the first day that they met. It just happened; as evening approached, Hannah could not resist. She dipped closer and closer to his surface with each passing moment. It was as if gravity pulled them toward each other, a force rather than either's specific desire. Hannah turned from bright white to a tangerine orange with the heat of it all, until that irreversible moment when they at last touched. It was like an explosion across the sky, colors appearing everywhere like fireworks as they melded together, grew closer and closer until Charlie had managed to touch every surface of her.

It was like no other kiss in the universe. The entire night that they spent together felt perfect. So from that day on, Charlie awaited tumultuously, his waters churning chaotically as Hannah rose in the sky, getting closer and closer to him with each moment.

And each day she came. Every now and then there were clouds, fog, even rain between them. At first these things separating them drove Charlie crazy, devastated him. Oddly enough it was a little bit more exciting for Charlie, once they'd loved each other a while, when he could not see Hannah. He knew that eventually she would still dip below the clouds to plant a kiss on him tenderly, but this way he could not see her approaching.

It allowed him to imagine that things might be different.

This desire for difference, well, there was nothing wrong with Hannah. In fact, Charlie usually imagined that she was perfect. After a while, though, he simply desired something new, something more exciting than this routine they'd fallen into.

Little did he know, Hannah had taken to these feelings even more intensely. Every time they touched, he was still cool and refreshing, smooth and strong as he surrounded her, but she was accustomed to it.

To be frank, she had grown bored.

Boredom became a sickness that progressed awfully quickly. The speed with which she fell in love with Charlie was nothing compared to the speed with which those feelings slipped away from her. She tried to hold on, gripped with her fiery fingertips. For a while, when they kissed she kissed him harder. Summer seemed to approach in the dead of winter, because Hannah's only solution to this loveless predicament seemed to be to heat up.

When Charlie saw how hard she was trying, though, he became discouraged, because he realized that he on his own was not enough to inspire her love. And his being discouraged made him seem colder, more distant. Fog rolled in for a series of weeks as these competing temperatures raged on.

One morning, as Charlie hopelessly lapped at his shores, though, no fog rose from his surface. He sloshed about in confusion, wondering what the sudden cool temperature was about. There Hannah was, creeping over the dunes. Only, she looked smaller than usual, up in the sky.

For a brief moment he basked in the distance, enjoyed the space. Water rushed almost all the way to the dunes as Charlie sighed in relief. The sigh felt wrong though at the foamy edges of his waves.

Just as quickly as he had found relief, Charlie was in despair. Perhaps he only wanted what appeared to be something he could no longer have, or maybe he was just afraid of change, but he grew nauseous with the fear of losing Hannah. The queasiness rose, gaining momentum as it rushed up in him from his ocean floor.

Hannah could hardly look on as a tsunami surged forth. She knew the pain that she was causing him in those last few moments. And all the while she was growing smaller and smaller up in the sky when she ought to have been getting closer to him. She told herself that her pain amounted to just as much as his, though, as endless gallons of water slowly retreated back into Charlie.

She felt so cold as she slipped further into outer space. When she could not even imagine how cold Charlie must be feeling. Without their love, though, she was growing dim along with distant.

The other stars cried out at Hannah, told her to return. They asked, if it hurt so much and she loved him so much, then where was she going?

Hannah was not sure that she could explain the way that things could never go back. She murmured some half-hearted reasoning for why she and Charlie could never return to the love they had, but they did not understand. At her blazing core, though, she was entirely certain that slipping back into place would never feel right again. They'd hurt each other too much in those few faltering moments where their love had faded. He would never look at her again without thinking of pain.

"Hannah," he calmly called in a roll of crashing waves.

"If I kiss you again it'll only hurt."

As he pulled inward on himself, disturbing the tides as he grew deeper and infinitely less wide, Hannah seized the moment as her best shot. If she waited any longer, she'd puff into a small cloud of smoke only to disappear forever in the pain.

So in one grand burst of energy, much more quickly than the way she'd been fading out of this atmosphere until then, she thrust herself out into the universe.

The world around Charlie grew instantly dark; night took over before Hannah had set. His eyes flashed desperately at the sky overhead, scanning the millions of stars. One of them was Hannah, he knew, but before he could pick out one to hope over, he froze.

Without her warmth, all of her love, he became suspended in icy pain.

Hannah's light faded. Even if she did return to her solar system, she could never produce enough heat again to unfreeze Charlie. She told herself this, but somehow even that knowledge was not enough to excuse her, enough for her to allow herself to grow fiery and burn red ever again.

# The pond that could pretend

Dedicated to Haley Walker

Charlie was erratic, could rarely be counted on. He brought what was expected of him to the table, but never stuck around to see things through. Don't be too quick to judge, though; some simply are not capable of commitment or thinking about the long term.

Despite his inability to think of what lay ahead, he was always onto the next thing, always zipping from place to place. Everywhere he went, he trailed excitement in his wake. That was Charlie's most redeeming quality; he was abuzz with energy all of the time.

This too he could not be blamed for, for it was also in his nature. Nothing less could be expected of a bundle of electrons like Charlie. It would be cruel to ask him to slow down or take his time, for him to feign preoccupation. For Charlie's sake, then, we'll have to change our view.

For a moment pretend that time does not exist.

Under this assumption, Charlie is a lot easier to understand. Charlie and Hannah were introduced when Charlie plummeted at the speed of light out of the sky above. He'd been bouncing around up there anxiously for quite some time, buzzing amidst the clouds. It makes sense then how severely he shocked Hannah when he collided with her, because he was wildly excited to finally escape the sky and all of that pent up energy hit her in a lightning bolt.

His mind moved quickly, and so this chance to encounter something new, anything new, left him thrilled. The joy bursting from him at the edges like light, it was enough to instantly grab Hannah's attention. She was captivated by something so excited about existing, so full of energy, so refreshing.

Hannah was not nearly as excited about things as Charlie was. She knew this about herself, knew that she tended to let things pass through her without much of a response. The way she saw it, though, she was just calm, and calm was the way ponds ought to be anyhow. Her calm, it meant she was at peace with the world around her. She didn't need much more than the sun warming her surface in the day and the moon reflecting off of her fish's scales at night.

Yet in the instant that Charlie struck her, when his lightning bolt reflected off of her surface instead of the sun or the moon, in the moment that they loved and in the moment that they became forever changed, she craved so much more than peace. Suddenly, Hannah was excited too. Like usual, she let him move through her, electrocuting every centimeter of her, inside and out. This time, though, she was all response. She lit up and came alive as much as Charlie did.

In the grand scheme of things, this excitement and joy and the only feeling she'd ever known to call love lasted very briefly. Time is a rather subjective concept, though.

Hannah had never known someone so deeply. All she had to do was feel him, his shocks, and she knew of all of his journeys and all of his encounters. She could feel him and know that he had travelled through thousands of other water particles, and that he had never felt this way about another.

Maybe it was the way he lit up even more for her. When he should have been losing energy to her as he weaved through her, he only grew brighter and emitted more. He gave her his all.

And Charlie was certain that he knew her enough as well. As he ran along the curves of every molecule, threw Hannah's most basic structure out of whack with his touch, it was like he had never been without her. He almost had the urge to slow down, to settle into her depths and bathe himself in her coolness forever. Charlie, with an electric tongue, whispered words that had to have travelled at a thousand syllables per minute, words that she had not even realized she had been waiting her whole existence to hear.

If love is felt deeply enough, perhaps, then it does not need to last forever, doesn't need to last for very long at all to leave its mark. Maybe Hannah could survive forever living on the intensity, even only of that briefness, which they had felt. For that moment she had wanted infinitely more, and yet he had pumped that infiniteness through her watery veins as he raced across every plane of her. So maybe she could be satisfied enough with only that one moment of love.

"I love you too."

And so it was done; she had gurgled the words in a series of tiny bubbles. She had doomed herself forever to waiting, she realized, as Charlie burst through her surface and sent one final pulse buzzing across her water skin. His absence instantly ached.

She shook for a moment, as the light that he had injected into her faded down into her depths, down to her muddy floor where it dissipated, and she too settled again. Hannah lay there thinking, feeling, absorbed in every spot on her where Charlie had left an afterimage. She could still see him everywhere, even as she sank into herself, into the darkest part of herself. He did not fade.

Yet Hannah was not sad exactly. She was not sad knowing he had probably coursed back up into the atmosphere, or perhaps along her shores, through wind currents, or even other bodies of water. She was just sure that he would come back to her.

Because how could she have felt the way that she did, how could he have said those things, how could he have felt that same way, if he were not someday coming back? And she was certain he had felt it, too, because she'd seen him grow brighter.

So, he would return.

Charlie told himself that he might return, too, when he was ready. If he slowed down, was brought down a few energy levels, well then maybe he could find his way back to Hannah and be reunited with the pond that he had so unexpectedly and deeply fallen in love with.

It wasn't at all that he didn't love her. Love just was not his forte. Charlie had so much more in the world that he had to do, so many reactions to ignite and engage in. Maybe if he was satisfied with those, then one day he would tumble back into Hannah's awaiting arms.

Until then, though, she would encircle and swirl around those afterimages, shadows, memories, hold onto what was only an instant in the grand scheme of things. She almost began to cry, to sob and leak watery streams at her edges, when she thought of how long this suffering of sorts, this waiting, might go on. The trail he had traced across her watery heart felt like an open wound, a path where she had been cut out and only a hole remained. She filled the emptiness with her coldest waters, felt the stinging as it grew icy. She almost felt sorry, knowing that her fish were suffocating as she agonized and that the strange currents so new to her were probably tearing up the plants that grew along her floor. The idea of time contaminated her and cut into her like acid would.

So.

For a moment pretend that time does not exist, she told herself.

# We feel empty before we've been full

Dedicated to Adrian Contreras

Cold is simply the absence of heat. It is the vacated space which energy, which warmth, has left behind.

Imagine the coldest thing, the iciest touch, which you have ever felt. You might imagine a gust, a sensation, which resembles Charlie. Embrace him and feel as he digs into you, bites at the surface of your skin until you are awash with numbness. Yet, somewhere below that surface you are still stumbling amongst pins and needles of cold. This is the pain that is his existence.

Because Charlie, as cold is the absence of heat, he is the absence of Hannah.

He can imagine her, at least. In his blustering, windy and chaotic excuse for a mind, he can produce a replica of her touch. Yes, Charlie has the capacity to know of warmth, but only by hearsay.

She is fast, ridden with energy, abuzz with light. She can be sweltering and full and cause those around her to become sluggish. Just as well, though, she can ignite the lives of others. She can bring them back to life from a cold and barren numbness.

Hannah, like a nervewracking goddess with unruly hair and thick, creamy thighs and a smile that stuns, can make you sweat.

Charlie knew all of this, but he had not experienced it himself.

It made him crazy, drove him to a madness which howled into the night, calling her name and every name in search for relief from the cold.

Despite the fact that Charlie himself was an overwhelming emptiness, he always dreamt of more. He always saw himself as fit to be full. It was oxymoronic; he was so ready to be full of heat, ready for love, ready for Hannah, that he inherently deterred her. Love never catches you when you're waiting for her, his breezy friends often said. Still, Charlie was always in anticipation.

Perhaps it was his capacity for imagination that made him so cold, so gapingly empty.

Because when he closed his eyes he would swear that he could feel her.

He was becoming jaded, though, a bit hopeless. For he had met so many Hannahs, and none of them were the true thing, none were honest, sincere, fiery heat. They were imposters, mere sensations, perhaps a chemical burn or a spicy scent in the air. Hannah, though, she illuded him.

There were warm gusts, breezes, out there though, Santa Annas that swept the hillsides and melted warmth into grass, into the Earth, into the organisms there. So it had to exist for him someday. He simply could not be condemned to absence forever.

He had mistaken others for THE Hannah three times by then. They'd been beautiful, and they'd felt good as they expanded to fill the cavernous cold that he could only call his heart. They were intense times, these times when he'd repeatedly thought he'd found her. He felt full at last, only to discover that infatuation could never match love, that unlike love it was hollow, eventually disintegrated only to leave him shuddering against the iciness again.

He'd travelled corridors, swept over seas, weaved through clouds, all chasing these potential Hannahs. And only to arrive at disappointment when he found the infinite ways that their loves were lacking. He swam in the flaws, immersed himself, because he was certain she was out there and he just could not settle.

Three times he let them go and three times he felt a little colder afterward.

When he looked up at the sun, he knew she was there. The mere glimpses, brushes of warmth from those rays, they would hardly compare to the heat of Hannah, he told himself. She would overrule him, overheat him, leave him awash in warmth and near begging for relief, for the cold again. She would fill his void and leave him always happy, burning up.

Charlie wandered the planet this way, plagued by an idea. She was a disease of his mind, an image that had been born of stories, retellings of others' experiences that he just had to take at face value because, well, they sounded like the most wonderful thing in the world. He persisted with this idea because love sounded like the best feeling, the highest high.

It wasn't until one afternoon, after yet another Hannah which had only briefly sated the longing for heat, intensity, and wholeness, that he began to wonder. This particular Hannah had been smooth and easy, caressed his vacant surfaces softly and murmured summertime words as she kissed him, and somehow all of this rightness had made him cynical and angry.

Because she was so right, felt so right and looked so right and sounded so right as the sweet nothings spilled from her temperate lips. Yet he still felt empty.

If this was not Hannah then who the hell was!

He pushed her away because he could not stand himself, his emotions, and was disgusted with his ability to touch her when he knew the love was not there. There was no use denying it, though; she simply was not Hannah. The cold seemed to burn this time.

At last, Charlie condemned himself. It was not the Hannahs, he decided, not their inability to warm him at all. No, the problem was Charlie, his incessant vacancy that clearly could not be filled. He decided, that night, that he simply was not capable of love.

After time in recluse, time tumbling in the cold, Charlie went numb. He didn't feel the hole in him, or, the hole that he was. It was almost as if he wasn't even cold anymore.

That was, until he felt something which could contrast it, someone who could bring light to just how cold he'd become. Right when you don't expect it, you might find the warmth you've been waiting for.

# We talk without hesitation

Dedicated to Dylan Andrews

You have a conversation with someone, starting with a measly exchange of words. "Hi, my name's Charlie. Where are you from?" "A grove quite far away." "I travelled pretty far to get here, too." And it starts that way and all of a sudden you feel as though you're in love.

That conversation becomes a deadly condemnation. Because, like Hannah, you could land on that off chance that you really, truly like them.

Surrounded by a sea of petals, other tiny flowers which had gingerly floated along breezes or simply wavered from the surrounding trees down to the grassy floor, Hannah could suddenly only see Charlie. And likewise she had entirely captured his eye. Other flowers arrived on the air or even floating down the stream nearby, and the pair was churned by passing dear and flighty birds, but what had begun as a conversation was becoming a liking.

Charlie's petals were not particularly bright, and Hannah's pollen could not catch the sunlight quite right, but it was the words, those words, the way they rolled off her petals like extended pink tongues. With each phrase, since that first handshake, they moved closer. And they'd only just met, but they'd started a flower dance conversation, broken stems swaying and leaves blustering like a strange sign language until they were swaying to the same rhythm, petals flustered in the same pattern.

She smiled at him and felt as if she'd known him for much longer. He consoled her and said he'd found her beautiful since the moment she'd settled in the grass.

This was not petty conversation, only necessary that they brush the surface when they'd already delved so deep. They shared about their ever-present desire for sunlight, their shared passion for whispering when the wind passed by. Hannah could feel all the things that they did not have in common, a bit abrasive in the heat of the afternoon, but they hardly mattered when she'd just met Charlie in this clearing, this sea of flowers, and they already shared so much.

You start a conversation with someone and you get excited. Charlie just couldn't stop smiling. He admired every word on her soft lips. And he wanted to weave his green fingertips through hers and found himself wondering what it might be like to press petal to petal in a tender kiss.

Except it was not an intense desire, not a need like passion, because he was having a conversation with her.

You get excited for things to come, though, thinking maybe you'll keep on murmuring through your flower mouths. Maybe you'll get a waft of his distinct pungent scent one afternoon, maybe you'll remember these flower feelings pulsing through your xylem and phloem that are so illogical but which feel so good that you can't suppress them. So you keep up the conversation when there's nothing left to say. Hannah liked to ask questions; it was easy and she was interested. And it was nice because he asked them back.

Because they were starting to like each other and starting to care about each other. Although she'd noticed him from that first moment, admired his shape and his smile, well it wasn't until later that she caught the ever-pleasant, friendly, that happy glint in his eye. Hannah found herself wishing she wouldn't have to say goodbye.

You start a conversation with someone and it seems harmless. Because, let's face it, under normal circumstances you aren't going to click with most, if any, of the flowers you simply encounter. Every now and then, though, you might end up like Hannah and Charlie.

So for a while they kissed, but they always kept up their conversation. And then the wind picked up and Hannah, with a bittersweet sigh, told Charlie it was time to say goodbye. He rode the breeze with her for a while, but was not ready to leave the grove. And so they kissed one last time and Hannah told him, "I'm so glad I met you," because, after all, all she'd done was meet him.

Yet there was a strange feeling at her center when this stranger was gone and Hannah felt something like a longing, but also something like hope and excitement, as she drifted down to the surface of some far off stream, awaiting something, though she wasn't sure what yet.

Maybe she ought to ask someone, but of course that would entail beginning another conversation. The spots on the tips of her petals where she'd grown a bit brighter with Charlie, well, despite their beauty they reminded her of the dangers of beginning a conversation. It may leave you elated, but who's to say you won't find yourself wanting more?

# We feel distant until we're no longer close

Dedicated to Nicole Craft

You are the imperceptible ripple along the surface of water, the vibration against a standstill surface, the disruption of molecules in the air all around you. You are a sound wave, and Hannah loves you.

She, unfortunately, has also become certain that you are the one.

You can remember the first time she heard you whispering in her leaves. It was hardly intentional, just a passing by, and sure you noticed the smoothness of her lush greenery and the curves of her thick bark, but she was just another tree amidst a forest. It was not until she murmured back that you paused, quit reverberating and listened for just a moment. It was not something you were used to.

Her words were so sweet, though, Charlie, that for once you ceased speaking. Rather than grow onward, you grew wide, encircling Hannah in ringlets of sound like the gray ringlets which you could imagine encircling her heart beneath that soft but dense bark. You reached from the very tips of her tear shaped leaves to the stringiest lengths of her roots. You tasted the sour sap that gushed from where she'd been cracked and the gossamer stickiness of the spider webs that stretched along her branches.

Once she'd snagged you, really caught your attention, you were enthralled. The funny thing about Hannah was that she was so intent on retaining the coolness that kept her leaves so green and her trunk impenetrable. She was not at all interested in embracing such feelings. She'd gotten used to stretching deep into the Earth, rooting around for cool water when she was sad, and reaching up with her leafy fingertips toward the sky when she felt inspired. She did not particularly have time for you when you first stopped.

You knew she liked you, though; otherwise she'd never have started the conversation, exhaled droplets of water from her stomata to catch you mid-wave. With faith that she cared for you, you collapsed into love. This was the first time you'd sang for only one.

Hannah had never been much for the other trees, kept her decaying leaves and soft pink blooms to herself. She settled easily into your melody, too easily, with no hesitation and no distractions. She wasn't about to admit that she was in love, but she let you ring through her leaves and chatter amidst her branches.

You were ready to breech her bark, at least after a while.

Hannah was not one to let things in. She was firm against the wind, cautious with the sun, hesitant with other organisms as they caressed her edges or at least begged some kind of entrance. It was in her nature to be closed off.

You wanted to ring against the tiny hollow spaces inside, though, peak into the spaces between. It's possible that you wanted to feel close, craved that fairytale feeling that you'd sometimes felt move along you, along just the right harmony. You wanted to feel like you were intertwined, like you'd never let go and like there was something between you so intense that there was nothing between you at all. For however much Hannah let on, you knew there was more to her. You wanted to reverberate along each ring until you could touch that core. You were certain no one had ever touched her heart before.

With this knowledge, why did you think it was your place to? Thick bark implicates a tender core. Why else would it be there?

You got close regardless, so close that she could feel you leeching in like a nutrient or a poison and becoming one with her every fiber. She began to turn pink on the inside, her rings a deep maroon, everywhere that you managed to touch her.

And you didn't get far. It's not like she felt close to you, and for that matter you to her. But something had changed.

So when your rhythm began to irritate her and your song became too loud for her tree vessel to contain, when you slipped quietly from between the stems of her leaves and told her you'd be back, that you needed space, needed to see the sky for a while before you were ready for what was to come, she did not hesitate to let you go.

It was only when you were gone that she felt the spine crackling pain, the impending crisis of a broken structure, because once you'd sneaked inside, Hannah had been compromised and her trunk had grown porous and she'd begun to sink into the ground. You watched from a distance as she melted into the earth, one inch at a time, decomposing little by little, and suddenly looking in from the outside you felt so close.

What you take for granted, what you're willing to sacrifice or leave behind; what you tell yourself you've forgotten and what you had always felt a certain distance from, a space in between keeping you separated, well it feels close now, but only because you're far apart.

# We feel wrecked under false presumptions

Dedicated to Lorri Greene

How do you tell someone that they've ruined you? Well, you don't; if you have even an ounce of strength, you don't stoop that low. But you want to.

You want to look them stone cold in the eyes and murmur those words, half in that love voice you used to reserve just for them and half in a tone of pure resentment. Then, you want to hold that stone expression as they fumble for some way to explain that such a thing is impossible, that they don't have such power over you, or at least never intended for things to go so wrong. You won't, though, you won't maintain that cool. You know that once the words are out you're bound for breaking, crumpling, spilling into an avalanche of tears and pain because, after all, they've ruined you. And what's worse, despite this ruining, you still desperately love them.

Charlie wondered how he might tell Hannah that she ruined him without such a pathetic outcome. He wanted her to know; perhaps he wanted to hurt her by bestowing upon her the knowledge of the wreckage she'd caused. Pain breeds pain, he justified to himself. It was only natural that he craved her hurt. Then they could heart ache in unison, there would be a bit of togetherness again. He wondered if she would care, the wild current that she was, so suddenly preoccupied with her own existence that it was possible she would not be phased at all.

When they were together, he was her everything.

Then again, when they were together Charlie was a roaring waterfall. And what was he now? A pathetic trickle, a measly mumbling of water down the face of somehow still slick rock. She had transformed him from a powerful crashing of bountiful, cool water into a pathetic excuse for a downhill stream. Because she'd been his direction.

He figured if maybe she would just take the time to glance, to peek at him, well he wouldn't have to explain at all. It would be glaringly obvious. She, as was mentioned, was quite preoccupied, though, and frankly did not want to see. It was quite the pathetic decline.

So Charlie was forced to call out to her. Her name formed round on his water droplet lips as they dripped from the edge of rock and cascaded slowly, like rose petals, onto murky and near still water. Before, he had churned the water.

Just as she was not looking, Hannah was determined that she was not listening either. She rationalized it as a chance to spare him pain. But Charlie was certain that this was her selfish way of avoiding her own agony.

Hannah swayed along some stream, headed she did not know where. All she knew was that she could not be with Charlie.

How could she tell him that he'd ruined them?

Because Charlie had rushed with such force and gone and shattered what little heart she'd had, and then he'd churned up the pieces, splintered her until she had a heart as fine as sand. From that, perhaps she could've recovered. Maybe in the heat of their love the little pieces would have melded and formed glass. And sure, a glass heart would be fragile and he'd have to be careful with her, but at least they'd be together.

There was no possibility of such a fate even, though, because Charlie had stepped further. He'd run along edges of that rock he never had before and picked up poisons in her shattered heart absence. His water was so far from pure then.

Hannah tried, she tried to look upon him the same way. But the poison tinted his water, and his kisses never tasted the same. She tried to explain gingerly that he'd wrecked their love, but Charlie was never one for accepting.

She fled, and years later he still begged the question, how do I tell her she's ruined me? And all Hannah could think was, Darling, you've ruined yourself.

It wasn't until he decided that he didn't love her that water began to fill him again. And he decided it was not a poison, either, only a change in coloration. What did he need her approval for anyway, when there were other currents rushing past with each season? So Charlie settled into the acceptance that, yes, he'd loved her; but their love was no longer.

It, of course, did not stick.

In general, he held fast to this proclamation. There were moments of weakness, though, moments when water faltered and he felt ruined again, when he felt small.

She was right in that effect, though, that he'd ruined himself. For their love had been plenty powerful, but Charlie was his own water entity, surrounded by possibility, and strangling himself to a sad excuse of a stream was an excuse in itself. He was certain, then, that he wanted to roar.

# We feel lost when we're not loved

Dedicated to Walter Kanzler

It would be easier than this. That's a pretty bold statement, too, considering. It makes this out to be beyond a nightmare.

Worse than a nightmare, you just can't sleep. You don't toss, you don't turn. You simply lie awake, and on this particular night you stare up at the moon from this sandy spot you've landed, pondering how it would be easier.

It would be easier, despite any pride or self-respect that you have left, Hannah, to beg and plead and grovel and cry and sacrifice your resolve and become that pathetic, needy piece of driftwood that you promised yourself you would never be, than lying here in the agony of having lost Charlie. Because Charlie was, though not your everything, everything that you loved for a while. He was your vessel, your heart, your home.

Hannah and Charlie met at a young age, when Hannah came crashing down from some tree and rather than colliding violently with the shore below, he caught her. He cradled her in soft lullaby waves until she knew no other rhythm. Perhaps that was how he snagged her so resolutely. His tides moved her just right, because Charlie was a gentle ocean, but his rolling waves kept the whole thing exciting.

She fell in love so quickly. And with an intensity none other could compare to.

Charlie himself could not deny that it was an unhealthy love. He could feel himself compromising her, filling her in and turning her soft where once she'd been strong. Her outer layer peeled, and at first this seemed wonderful, it seemed like vulnerability and openness, but evidently was Hannah losing her sense of self. She was breaking apart into Charlie's arms, giving herself to him much too entirely, and he had no idea how to stop it.

He continued to kiss her goodnight and roll her into his waves, his foam and his cool turquoise.

Hannah also thrived on their love. For however much she was losing herself, she had plenty to gain. Each morning as the sun warmed her carbon fibers and Charlie rocked her back to wakefulness, she discovered a new side of their love.

They appeared all along her skin.

First plants that latched onto her, algae, and then little creatures that expressed their love, barnacles and mollusks and eventually even a bright orange starfish. He was becoming a part of her too.

Yet all the closeness was weighing her down.

He'd had a hard enough time watching her be compromised, but this? This was too much. Hannah, no longer drifting, but sinking into his depths.

With no warning, he went wild one night, not with rage but with sobs and tears and a deep swaying sadness, until one final wave carried her like a gentle tsunami far onto some distant shore. It was his way of saving her, but also of saving them, because deep down their love had begun to make him feel sick. So he rushed around her in a foamy, bubbling burst and thrust her away, in what seemed like cruelty, but what was out of some kind of love. Because he couldn't love her anymore.

And then he retreated. That was infinitely more cruel.

It would have been different if Charlie somehow managed to carry her home, back to her tree, or perhaps if he'd warmed her up to the idea of abandonment. But instead he simply thrust her away, love barnacles and all, onto some dry, blazing shore where all she knew how to do was remember. In the quiet where she could sometimes here the rolling of his tongue as he crashed against rocks and sand, it seemed all she could do was remember.

And this, she learned quickly how to exist in this. That is, if that's even possible.

Learning how to live always heartbroken may very well not be possible, but that depends on how you define living. Hannah wasn't sure if she was living anymore.

Maybe that's why it would be easier, then, easier to plead that he take her back, or that the moon tug on his tide, or that the wind thrash against her painfully until they be reunited.

Easier, though, does not always imply better, and Hannah realized this one day on her soggy bed of sandy tears. She realized that she would not be returning to the sea anytime soon. Hannah had to learn how to live without Charlie if she was going to learn how to live at all. It might be easier to rush back into Charlie's arms, but then who would she be? She would be Charlie's again, but could she also belong to Hannah? Perhaps not.

# We sleep without fear of

# waking

**Dedicated to Dale Gottdank**

Every single time, you forget. It's torturous. But each day, when the sun first rises and you feel the tingling of heat creeping into all of your tree trunk wrinkles, when you can at last see again, you are disappointed by what you do not see, by what you've forgotten.

It's a nightly hibernation, and you're awoken to an entirely altered world. A world without Hannah. It hits you like the sharp end of an axe tearing into your very foundation, every single time.

It should be getting easier, you think. But sleep causes you to forget. In your dreams there she is. And your sleeping mind expects, every morning, to see that light, rather than pouring from the sky, reflected brilliantly off of her glistening white surface. Even when you don't dream of her, the misconception is there. You forget that the bed of snow that you so fell in love with melted away, abandoned you and left you hot and sweaty in the springtime humidity.

She's gone, you remember now. Like every other morning you feel yourself crack internally. You're breaking. Your branches sag and your new sprouting leaves are emerging yellow instead of their usual healthy green. Even in her absence, you are lovesick. Yes, it's worse in her absence. Because in her absence the snowflakes which made up Hannah are purely an idea and how lovely an idea can be.

In your mind, waking or dreaming, all you see is perfection. You see the purest white and such geometric flakes and a flat surface that insulates the sleeping Earth around you. You remember her touch, shocking with its harsh cold yet still so gentle and smooth as she rested against you. Here, in your head, she's wonderful. Here, on the Earth, she's gone.

The worst bit is that you have no one to blame. You can't even blame her for the gut wrenching pain, the agony that seems to twist your internal fibers and wring them, wring them dry of all hope or joy. You can't blame her because it was all about timing.

You knew it was coming too. If anyone is to blame for your pain, it's you, Charlie. Springtime was always on the calendar.

So how were you surprised when she was depleted, the distance between you growing greater? It was for your own good that she began to pull away, melt away in that reflective sunlight. She was sparing you, sparing you the true pain of springtime when she'd be rushed down the mountain and out of your life forever. No snow before had ever felt to you like Hannah did, not as deep, not as refreshing.

It was the way she found such purpose. She found fulfillment simply in loving you. Loving you deeply and piling more and more for days, Hannah, if not the biggest blizzard you'd ever seen, was certainly the most impressive, the gentlest, careful not to tear through your branches, and with her starlike snowflakes the most beautiful.

Two entities in love are easily lost in it. Charlie, clearly, was so lost in it. It feels so good that you pretend there are no consequences. And then here he is waking up every morning to the groan and moan of loss. This year, Charlie's blossoms emerged pale white instead of pink. They did not bloom even, only remained buds and then crumpled, drifted. He couldn't muster the energy for springtime, not in this mourning.

The forgetting is a curse. Sometimes Charlie wonders if he ought to not sleep at all, if only to spare himself the pain. How many days and nights can pass by awake before you lose yourself to a crazed sleepiness, degenerating into an excuse for existence?

Yet he would almost rather hardly exist at all than start each morning this way, than exist in ever-present pain.

It always gets better. As the day progresses on, the knowledge settles onto him like a sickly sweat, always feeling disgusting and awful, but at least it dries eventually. And after a while he can become distracted enough to not even notice how bad it hurts. After all, it is springtime.

Birds chatter in his emergent leaves, grass wraps around his protruding roots (a bit like the way that she did), and the sun and the breeze usher in new life. It rains all the time, those spring showers, and the spatter would be refreshing if only everything didn't remind him of her. The water droplets are a sorry excuse for the kisses she once bestowed on him. Still, it gets better. As the day goes on, the acceptance makes it better.

By the time it's night again, he feels strong. He questions how he ever hurt so badly over something as cold as Hannah. He hardly even misses her sunrise sparkle. By the time it's night again, he's confident that he'll do just fine without the sun, he'll maintain his mind and wake up feeling fine.

Nighttime always plays this trick on him.

He wakes up again with branches extended to meet her as she cascades like soft white angel feathers from heaven. He wakes up again with roots reaching to wrap around her and caress every surface of her cool and slick skin. He wakes up wanting only to kiss her.

And he is plunged into the pain all over again, when it is all unattainable. From now on, he figures, he'll be better off to simply never sleep, because to never sleep, well he'd evade the risk of dreams, the risk of his poor, twisted mind conjuring those love feelings again. Awake, he could be sure, there would be no more love feelings for a while.

# We feel eager before we feel ready

Dedicated to Alison Croty

You're so ready to be in love again. You are so ready. It's this deep ache that starts in your chest and sinks, sinks and rests in the center of your belly.

From time to time, you insist to yourself that it's true love you crave because, and this must be true, you've never really been in love before. No, that could not have been love, you think, because you need some solace. You can't admit to yourself that you fell so hard for Charlie. Or, what's worse, that he could still be the cold you're craving.

No, certainly not. This is an ache for true love. Perhaps it will feel similar to the way things did with him, but it must be different. Of course you'll crackle again, your structure will be entirely re-aligned. You'll go from a boring, watery, prism of a blob, to a glittering, skeletoned snowflake. That's what happens to water droplets who fall in love.

.

You want to feel that crackling along your emergent spine. You want to feel like you'll glitter again and catch the light, not with a circular reflectance, but with one riddled with angles and sharp turns. You want to scatter light. Most of all, though, beyond all of those things that you'll feel with regard to yourself, oh you want to feel cold.

You're ready to escape warmth, and along with warmth ready to escape boredom. Is that what the ache is? Are you burning up in the boring heat?

Boredom is no motivation to seek love, though, and you know that Hannah. It's just that you haven't felt anything, anything at all, in quite sometime. Your washed out life lacks excitement, joy, revelation, but also fear, angst, and sadness. It's possible that you've forgotten how to feel altogether.

You're certain, though, that if you press your lips against enough cold fronts you'll feel the sparking of crystallization again. You'll feel something again!

This is fear.

You're afraid to put yourself at risk again. In fact, it feels like laying your life on the line, or, it is. Because when

Charlie left Hannah almost died. The heat of the pain was so intense, and it wasn't just that she lost her shape and her skeleton surfaces, but she almost lost herself altogether.

Hannah had begun to evaporate when he was gone. Little by little, with each passing moment outside of his cold, cloud love, she was losing herself. Like a crazed fever, she was burning up from the inside and disintegrating. And she could not muster the strength or motivation to stop it. That was a very different ache; the ache of love loss could have killed her, left her so ill with sadness that she did not mind the idea of giving up and getting lost, scattered in evaporated bits in the sky, never to be Hannah again.

And what was this ache compared to such a thing? This desire had no chance of killing her. Although it could make her crazy and heat her up, it lacked one vital ingredient: here, alone, basking in solitude and entirely lacking love, there was no pain. There was just nothing.

With such risks in mind, why did she still find herself boiling? She's admitted two waves of sensation so far: the ache of desire, the ache of loss.

But Hannah also knew how impossibly wonderful it felt, even if the previous, that long-lost love, could never have been true because certainly it must get better than that, even despite that, she knew how tremendous it felt. That knowledge fueled the desire, but it was not always aggressive.

At times she simply basked in the joy of it, in the sweet feeling that ran along her snowflake limbs like dopamine coursing through veins. The feeling of a slow and cautious kiss. Or the feeling of a spontaneous and passionate kiss, icy so high up in the sky. The feeling of embracing, and the way such a feeling would never leave her regardless of Charlie's proximity so long as he continued to insist that he loved her. The comfort of being loved, the passion of loving another. She could hardly bear to think of it. Those thoughts ignited both fires, pain and desire.

How long had it been? Certainly long enough, enough time had to have passed. Hannah was growing impatient. She was so ready to love again. So at last, she laid her tear drop neck down on some metaphorical guillotine and she opened up again. Like the prism that she was, rainbows scattered around her as soon as she let light back in. And others saw her, as they'd seen her before, only now they too could see how ready she was.

Those colors were false advertising.

Anyway, she continued to be open, began blubbering water words again and smiling snowdrop smiles and extending watery fingers in every attempt to connect. It worked too well, really.

Because she was so ready that for moments she managed to deceive herself into thinking she was feeling it again. With each new face that garnered connection, she could swear it was building in her. Only, the flip between excitement and doubt began to take a toll. She would think, perhaps not directly but in some capacity, well I could see myself loving them, some other misty cloud. Moments later, though, it would hit her that, if not right, well it at least did not feel the same.

Why was she looking for similarity when she was so certain her Charlie love could not have been true? That there was something better?

Day by day she grew cooler, appreciating the time that was putting space between what had been and what was, and once or twice she even tested out the formulation of a new structure. She didn't realize it, but no two snowflakes are alike, and this uniqueness, it ached a little. She missed the familiarity of Hannah and Charlie.

Without him, though, the feeling could exist. Love could not be a one time thing, not entirely exclusive. Yet every time she tried and it felt, if only slightly, wrong, she cried off bits of herself in the heat of frustration. She was so ready. So why wasn't love awaiting her?

It wasn't the love evading her, though, it was her own inability to accept it. Like some foreign body, Hannah rejected these feelings which she so craved, because she was afraid of the little differences. Or perhaps she was afraid of the similarity.

From time to time she would play it out in her mind, the painful, hot disintegration that had plagued her before, only fresh and raw and to a new cold.

She shivered. Alone again, if only momentarily, in a gap between cloudy suitors, she was ushered back into the agony. She firmed up her edges, though, and insisted to herself that she was so ready. Love was hers to claim again. She needed it.

Then a raindrop friend, who saw her pain while cascading by, told Hannah that what she needed was not love, but time.

# We feel patient when time is our only hope

Dedicated to Hannah Septoff

Time is a curious entity. Although it may heal all wounds, it does not erase scars. They fade, perhaps resembling what once was, but time will never return things precisely to what they were. Not when things have changed.

So you feel the spot where you've been scarred. And the moss and flowers and greenery have returned, like scar tissue, attempting to fill the void. You look, and it's almost pretty, but you can still feel the pain there. And you look out toward him, and the pain is so much worse.

There's a biting competition, a fiery battle between the love you feel and the agony resentment. Someone who made you feel perfect. Someone who made you feel absolutely tragic. Someone who brought you to life, someone who metaphorically killed you.

And the attempt on your life is right there, embedded in the scar.

Forgiveness is just as curious. It often accompanies time. How much can you expect of forgiveness? Or, how much does it truly entail? Because someone's forgiving you does not erase their scars either, doesn't even fade them. If anything, it flaunts them in your face.

This is where you hurt me.

And it's okay.

But I'll never forget the way you hurt me.

Hannah did not have to say this to Charlie. It went unspoken but still said every time she looked out at him from her crystal quartz eyes. At first, Charlie thought maybe the glint would fade, like the scar in her rocky tissue had been filled, and that she could look at him with love again. This was a silly assumption.

Charlie clearly did not have that fundamental understanding of time. It was evident in that all he could say to Hannah, all he could say that last time they talked was "do you want me to wait for you? I'll wait for you. We have forever."

He did not understand how pointless forever was though. This was not a matter of the future, but entirely of the past, and the way that Hannah could never forget the rough spot where he had cracked through her surface and so carelessly grated against the most tender part of her.

Hannah thought for a while that she could forget. That was why she'd been asking Charlie for time, always time, until this moment.

Hannah had hope. She had hope for the nights when he'd scattered light across the sky to caress her faceted surfaces and kiss along her smooth curves. When he touched her then, after the hurt, there were moments when she imagined that it could feel the same. But then his light would just barely skim the scar and there she was at square one again, immersed in pain again, resenting and wanting to abandon the Charlie who had once seemed her one true love.

Someone you love. Someone you can't bear to look at. The memory of Charlie flashing through the sky, a beautiful lightning bolt full of energy and cascading molten love from above, challenging the more recent reminiscence of his ability to break things. Namely her hard heart, which had seemed so impenetrable before. When he'd come crashing through the sky that night, perhaps not with the intention of hurting her but still managing to rip her apart, well their love had changed. For Hannah, it was hardly love at all anymore.

You think you can wait an eternity for someone, because you love them enough to give up forever. Time, though, does not heal all wounds. That was obvious to Charlie when he offered one last time, "I'll wait for you."

And with pained eyes, Hannah replied, "I don't want you to."

# We feel in control until we've rescinded all rationale

Dedicated to Jill Clark

You never thought you'd kiss them. Having only known them momentarily, in that whole series of moments you never even saw an inkling of connection. Because they were great and all, interesting, funny, kind, and maybe they thought that about you as well.

So was it the context? You were sure that you just weren't their type. And they weren't exactly yours either, but they weren't NOT your type. Was it the submersion in a group? The way your eye contact was intimate, but infinitely friendly?

You just never saw yourself kissing them. And never imagined you might be pleasantly surprised. Never imagined that you might be thrust into the sort of situation you never foresaw with this particular individual.

That kind of tricky situation where you might say you're falling for someone. Perhaps that was why you never saw it, because they were so great that the prospect of liking them was really there. The prospect, but not the option. You didn't want to like anyone-- especially not someone here, now, in this moment. Because moments end and you're standing so close and thinking about how a day from now you'll be so far, they'll have evaporated and just disappeared like they'd never been there at all.

Only now does it feel natural and right. At first, their water lips looked too round to fit along the thin line that was your cautious mouth. You never imagined kissing. And now that they're up in the sky, 5,916 miles away, now is when it ironically feels right.

And suddenly Hannah couldn't get enough of him. She craved his vapor conversation, even from so up high, the same way she craved sunlight each day and her roots in the ground. When they shared conversation, it felt like he wasn't so far and from time to time she could imagine the shape of him as he rested against her, pressed up against her.

When in reality he was so far away.

Charlie really was out of her reach, and chances were she'd never see him again, never feel his cool edges again. Why had she gone and kissed him? Or worse, why had it felt so right!

Hannah was angry. Angry at herself for feeling again. Why couldn't it all be cold, all be the mere consequence of morning dew, water settling against her? That was her intention: only to feel while avoiding feeling altogether.

Charlie just had something to him and the moment he said he wished they'd kissed sooner, well, that something seemed like a little bit hers. So for a few moments they were as close as water and leaf can get, adhesion stronger than ever before. And then he was rushing off of her in such a hurry, gravity pulling them apart, and she knew that the morning sun was on its way to separate them for quite a while.

It seemed fitting that things had begun during nighttime.

And then Charlie was gone and, hell, she resented it. Simply resented the feelings.

The funny thing about Charlie was that she could not resent the dew drop himself for even a moment. Because every time he crossed her mind or she reminisced on their conversations, or worse their moments, or when he called down to her from the sky again, she felt nothing but good things.

When their conversation became serious, and she admitted that she hated the feeling things, she only felt closer to him. All 5,916 miles away, she felt closer when he too admitted he'd been hurt before. They bonded over being, if only slightly, damaged.

She liked really discussing though, even from afar. So she'd known he was great, but feared what he might reveal. Getting to know others, it always boded risky. And there he was spilling secrets and despite their intensity she found herself unaverse.

Hannah cycled through these feelings, between frustration at her inability to explore what was becoming of them further, anger at herself for allowing emotion in again, and, simultaneously, excitement at the sight of such feelings. It was a roller coaster.

That was, until one evening when he did not call back down from the sky.

She should have seen it coming, was stupid for feeling anything at all. The coaster came to a screeching halt after plunging down, down, down. Hannah felt sick, could feel her edges crinkling and browning in the dry heat. There was no water near to refresh her. No sight of Charlie.

And she realized there never would be.

It was not a loneliness, nor a mourning or sense of loss. Not when she'd only truly known him for a moment. He was gone, and Hannah was exhausted, so she wilted toward the Earth, and the soil caught her with open arms. It ought to not affect her so.

Charlie watched her, sort of sadly, as she disintegrated below.

And yet how many real words had they exchanged? He'd told her he'd visit if ever nearby, and he spoke with her from the sky above. But never had he suspected that the poor leaf could be falling in love.

You think that you expect the unexpected, that a mere emotion won't catch you in a trap like so. You think you know your thoughts and feelings, how you'll behave and that logic's on your side, but you never really know.

# We feel comfortable until we see the light

Dedicated to Zachary Kanzler

"No, I can't live without you."

And you sigh. You've heard this before. The same play every time. It's not like you're asking, not like you want an opinion.

You know what you need. That's all you've stated. And you're presented instantly with denial. Guilt.

"Don't do this," and it sounds like a command. You're so accustomed to listening, catering to every request and desire. When had you become passive? A slave to what you imagined was love?

The problem is you were never exposed to what love truly is. So a slave to being accustomed, craving familiarity. Whether it was love holding you there, well that comes into question.

But you're in denial too. Can't wrap your petals around the idea that you're not clever enough to see past this, that you're so susceptible to claims of love. You'd always taken yourself for a fairly smart moon flower, shutting your white flesh off in the daylight so no one could see inside.

Hannah, so up high in the sky, sneaked in though. And she knew how to keep you this way. She knew how to press your buttons. Somehow, all she had to do was ask you to stay.

Charlie, the poor flower, was constructed all too well. His stem reached up to her, tall. That's probably why she targeted him in the first place, targeted him as a victim of her love.

Not to mention he was kind. Much too kind for his own good. When she first wrapped her moonlight fingers through his petals, stamens, leaves, pistols, he was too timid to deny her entrance. Plus, she made him feel so bright. Charlie had never seen light before.

He mistook their light for love.

Love that seeps in and strangles, carries from the farthest point on your petals and reaches deep to your roots. It made him sick but she said this was the best medicine. Love that could kill because living always at another's fingertips means you may not be living at all. Charlie began to resent her.

It broke his heart that he was growing hateful. He wasn't that kind of flower. But she spilled at him such unkind words, "worthless", "cruel", "unloving", "unloved", that he could only bear to think them of her in return. What was love so contingent on pain?

"Hannah you hurt me."

And then she would justify. Explain. The passion of her love was what brought on those words. And then she'd grab with greedy moon fingers at his flower edges, seeking out his love in return. She was all need. Angry when he even bristled in the wind, when he did not want to kiss her good bye, when he wasn't quick enough to return an "I love you".

All need, she begged always more.

And he was so kind that he always offered.

Because Charlie didn't understand love, couldn't define the word.

When other flowers, flowers that looked on in the daylight, told him he was being manipulated, that it didn't sound like love at all, he defended. He could always describe the way she was so very light. She glimmered, at least to him, even deep in the night.

And he was comfortable in Hannah's arms. Her hateful words wrapped around him like a lullaby, wearing the masks which were the sweet words. Sweet nothings he realized. Nothing, embodied by her desperate need for love. But this was what he knew.

And when she said that she couldn't go on without him it felt like the world was crashing down. Not because he'd lose Hannah but because he'd be the cause of such tremendous loss. He could not claim that responsibility. Could not be the reason she might fall out of the sky.

After a while the defending was more for himself than anyone else. Had to remind himself. And this love was going, spiraling like tainted water down a rusted drain, going and it ought to be gone, but it dragged along with it a world of pain.

Because he'd never loved before and he'd also never lost. Despite the way she hurt him, when acceptance befell her crater eyes, he felt a little crushed.

"You can't do this," futilely, once more.

He almost believed her.

But this was a night built for goodbyes and just around the corner he could sense sunrise. So with careful precision he drew his petals back in.

"Good bye, Hannah," first love, worst hate, and never again.

# Offline

# We feel a void when drained of desire

Dedicated to Nicole Craft

You have no desire to be with them. This is it, end of the line. But you aren't looking back and it feels just a little bit odd to be accepting.

You've gone and said it yourself, though, no desire.

You've also accepted that you'll always desire the past. Always reminisce what was. But no desire to be with them in the here and now. Because you're strong and you've found your way and you know yourself now. Know what you truly want. Know what you truly need. Know that it isn't them.

And with all these things you know you're certain the feelings will follow. Even already, you have no desire to be with them. So it's working! No desire.

You can't even remember her name. Hannah was it? And you don't remember the smoothness of her bark or the smell when the wind washed through her leafy mane. Not in detail anyway.

You've forced the details out, blurred her image because then it's easier to look at. Bright green eyes. Gentle branchy smile. Easy rooted hips and fine, gray fingertips.

No desire.

Charlie hardly looks back on her for a second now. He's certain that he can, that it won't sting electric pain through every watery particle, it's just that he doesn't want to. Is choosing not to.

Because this was his choice.

No desire. Whatsoever.

Charlie had been the one to retreat, probably because he was the one capable. They both knew it was time. Had been too long. Together they were growing soggy.

And Hannah would have abandoned him long ago had it not been for her roots, those fibrous structures composed of insecurity and neediness that kept her at his side.

Charlie, though, was full of movement. And he saw in her branchy smile that the edges were etching away, she was growing worn. He wasn't about to stick around for their downfall. Wasn't interested in their demise.

So he was the strong one. He said good bye. Crackle. Pain like electricity stumbling on his water surface skin. Pain at the words good bye.

And yet no desire to say hello again.

Because he'd made the choice because he knew how wrong things had gone because she was getting distant because their love had become worthless because, because, because.

Give yourself a reason. That makes it hurt a little less. When you want someone but that someone is essentially dead, her trunk rotting on the inside and her once lush leaves cascading down.

They used to cascade to his riverbank edges. No longer. No desire.

He'd retreated despite her quiet protests. Wasn't ready for those two words. The electricity words. The words so necessary but which shock so harshly.

Why am I still thinking about this, he asks himself. He's strayed far enough from that shore so that he can't even see her anymore. And her image is so blurred. How could he still want her?

He knew what it would be if he gave in, returned. It would be forced kisses and stares crackling with pain behind the smiles. It would be fake laughs and too real cries. It would be everything that he left for.

And for that, he truly did have no desire.

You know what you desire, want, need. Except that all that desire is is for an absence. Absence of Hannah;

absence of dead and zombified love; absence of what had been. Now, how do you fill that void? How do you stop feeling empty when you desire nothing?

# We feel doubtful of the past while stuck in the present

Dedicated to Elisa Willes

Did they ever really love you at all? Feel even an inkling? Were the words a whole load of nothing? Were the meetings of eyes a lie?

It's hard for you to say, now.

Because logic would dictate that of course they must have loved you. After 16 months, 8 years, an eternity, 8 seconds; they must have. Who would waste their time like that?

Then you remember it's them and suddenly it seems reasonable. It seems reasonable that the whole bit was an act or a game or an experiment or simply an attempt to waste some time. And you seemed the perfect object upon which to waste time.

You feel queasy.

Queasy the way that Charlie's berries should have made others feel. That bright red color always a disguise for love. He wore the berries like adornment, and it wasn't until you tasted them that you realized they were a sweet lie.

Hannah, a nearby puddle, had been reflecting Charlie for quite sometime. She'd always laid in awe, staring up at his array of branches reaching so high and those beautiful, love colored berries. The ones which he insisted to others were poison.

Hannah was a mere puddle, down on the Earth, feeling always beneath him, despite the fact that as she evaporated she reached past him, past him up toward the sky. She couldn't see it, only saw Charlie's perfection. And in that, was certain that he could not truly love her. She doubted him then, but it was nothing like the way she doubted him now.

Upon first falling in love she took his words at face value. So when he started with yes, I like you, then, I've admired you for a while, she had to trust if she were to return the feelings. His leaves drifted down onto her surface and his scent began to tinge her water. This is what love does.

One day she asked about the bright love berries. And he hesitated, weaved around the question, came just this close to a lie. At last, though, he admitted they were all for show and that he could not really poison. And Hannah wondered briefly if likewise he could not truly love.

But Charlie kissed passionately and was insistent with his words. If for a second she expressed doubt, "sometimes I feel like-", he hushed her water lips with a kiss and that was that, all to be said. She couldn't keep the questions out of her head.

Eventually, 16 months 8 years an eternity 8 seconds later, she accepted that there must be something real.

Otherwise he wouldn't look at her with those big berry eyes. The ones that were a lie? Perhaps inherently but certainly not with regard to Hannah. She had to trust.

And that was her first big mistake. She let the love flow through her, let herself feel it and get lost in it and trust it. When she felt it so wholly, it was only inevitable that she come crashing down.

Deep in winter he left, the red love berries, poison berries, bosh berries, shriveled and turned black and cracked. They fell from his branches along with the rest of the leaves. All that was left was a bony skeleton, a memory.

Charlie left her and this framework was what she had to look back on. Only she could not fill in the spaces in between. Her memory was full of holes, perhaps holes where the lies had been.

And in retrospect the doubt consumed her.

It was reasonable in one further regard. Charlie had his acts and Charlie lived behind lies, but his true actions, those spoke loudest. The moment he said the love was gone, well he was gone, just like that, berries and all. Not a moment of hesitation. Not a second glance back.

If he'd loved her it couldn't be so easy. If he'd loved her there would be that one second of doubt. It propelled her into a much worse world of second guessing.

Funny, because it doesn't matter anymore. It doesn't matter even for a second what someone felt for you once they're truly gone. You have a hard time accepting that, though, you hold on tight, because to you it still means something which means it has to have meant something.

Sometimes you get caught up in the present, you see prospects of the future, and you smile at new days. You could care less if they loved you. You've accepted that you loved them once but no longer.

Except are they ahead in the game if they escaped Scott free and never even loved you at all? You ask yourself this and suddenly you're in the past again and obsessing on dead feelings again.

Because it isn't about a competition.

Not once your mind is really going.

No, then it's a hurling of your entire existence into pain because you loved so deeply, and does that make you a fool? Or worse were you unlovable in your not being loved?

Why did they inspire doubt in the first place, because you're somehow flawed? Worthless, easy to abandon, you are the poison to their berries.

The poison that infiltrated the love.

The love that now you're certain was never there in the first place.

You spiral and spiral through questions and always find yourself in this seasick place, begging the question, when things went so dreadfully wrong could he really have loved me at all?

# Untitled

Dedicated to Karen Martinez

Detritus. Your love is gone.

You've never lost someone before.

Once, someone you'd known only vaguely.

You could never call your love detritus. And here
you stand and you're murmuring the words detritus and then
screaming them and they're pouring from your lips and you
can't stop crying out, "detritus! Detritus! Detritus!"

You pause.

Your love is gone.

You go silent again, because your lips can't form
words. But more because there's nothing to say. How do you
process this situation enough to form one, single, coherent
thought, much less a word?

And it's still ringing through your head, detritus.

You're just glad you never murmured the words "til death do us part" because parting now would feel like losing everything. Oh right, you've lost everything.

Your mind races while still lying completely still. It's too cautious to make a move, to even attempt at thought. There's a risk that you'll go crazy with it. There's a risk that you already have.

Other mushrooms had mentioned this, had warned in vague and impersonal tales that death can leave you insane. Perhaps not permanently, perhaps infinitely.

Depends on the mushroom.

Depends on how you deal with things.

And you can't help but think, depends on who you've lost.

Another sob wracks your flimsy stem. The pores in your surface are too tight to let anything in, water, air. You're cracking on the surface and drying out. And you're ashamed because you've just truly learned what death is and here you are, thinking you're unafraid of dying. But a world without Charlie isn't worth living in.

You've experienced loss before, and you thought that was enough to suck the life out of you. The mere absence of love any longer, the sight of the one you love drifting away from you because things ended, that seemed like enough.

And now, now, drifting seems like a pleasantry. You would love to watch him drift away. You would cry with joy if he were merely making distance between you, not like the sorrowful sobs you cry now.

Now, you see the lightness of such a separation.

Because even if they're out of your life, well, they'll always be a part of your life as long as you can think of them and know that they're out there somewhere and still carrying a piece of your love. Now, that little light, if a dim and distant flame, well it's gone to blackness. Because now they aren't drifting. They're rotting.

Hannah had had thoughts like this when he initially left, when he drifted downstream away from her. She thought the whole world was ending when he wouldn't look at her with love eyes anymore.

At least then he had eyes at all.

Detritus.

Now he's resting on the ground. Your love is gone, she thinks to herself. And it had felt like it was gone for an eternity only now it's really gone, he's really gone, no chance of return, never to exhale sweet breath again, never to crackle in a breeze. His fate, now, detritus, is only to now truly become one with her.

Hannah embraced Charlie in death like she never had in life because in death suddenly every breath was significant. Every meeting of eyes. Every time he caused her pain and every time he brought her joy was nowhere to be found, because he didn't have a memory anymore.

He didn't have anything at all.

Wasn't anything at all.

Was detritus.

Your love is gone.

You had never pondered so deeply before, the idea of never growing again, soaking up sunlight again, rushing in the breeze again. These ideas seem mythical and distant. And there Charlie was right before you and that was his fate, that was his reality, was him right there, right then, never again.

It was selfish but you made it personal; he would never see again, but you would never get to see him. He would never plant a kiss again, but how could he notice? You'd be the one still around, still around in the hollow void, the absence, sucked into the vacuum space where he used to exist. This is Charlie's death, only right now it belongs to you.

Because you're the one who still feels the burn of not breathing. You're the one experiencing the individual cell death. You're the one absorbing every cascading feeling that seems to rush in and out like a sharp blade leaving you like

mincemeat, shredded on the inside.

And you wonder if you'll ever start breathing again.

# We feel insecure without

# shame

Dedicated to those who see their flaws

You want to be perfect. Not for you, for someone else. It's really quite selfless. You want them to see you, to hear you, to touch you, to perceive you, to think that you're perfect.

Then you'll get to feel perfect for a while.

Never mind that, though. You're sure it's entirely for someone else's benefit. That's the point of a relationship, right? To make someone else happy. Right, that's why you try.

You can tell yourself these things.

But you're really quite selfish with the way that you behave, always changing, changing for the benefit of Charlie.

It's in the nature of a shadow to be so subject to alteration. He moves in the sky and you warp to fit his position, his every desire. When he reaches center shot above, and you appear too tall, well just like that you've disappeared. You'll stay invisible forever for him. Because at this time of day, this way, you can momentarily feel perfect. But he's moving again and you have to keep up.

Now his day is getting longer. And he wants a shadow that stretches long too, dark and shapely against whatever surface you claim.  It's not like he asked you to be this way. Yet you can tell from the way he's always looking down at you.

Hannah forgot that it was all a mask for her inability to love herself. That was all right. She'd keep pleasing Charlie and the sky would turn out just fine. Twilight approaching, her moment of truth. All Hannah wanted was to feel perfect.

 For Charlie of course.

What was their love masked by a need for reassurance? Not love at all, Charlie was sure. That was why he hesitated in insisting, always, that she was just so. If he told her, well she'd only crave the approval more. And yet if he withheld it, well, dark clouds may loom and he could lose Hannah altogether.

Now why would he occupy his time with such an insecure shadow? Hannah was not always this way. From time to time she let go, curving and twisting around corners and uneven surfaces. She was playful and warped, she was fun. Charlie liked her dark laughter, and her bent smile. For every flaw, there was a counter and well he'd been chasing her across the sky for so long that he'd forgotten how to resist her on those breezy days.

And then there were those moments. The moments. The ones where none of it mattered and it was like Hannah was perfect, only without any of the trying.

They came every eve, just as he dipped down to touch the horizon and there Hannah was, so stretched out that she wasn't stretched at all and blending into the darkness. That was when he really saw her. And her silhouette was glorious only her silhouette didn't matter at all because it was the way she so gingerly kissed him that he gave up that final sunshine smile and set for the day, set himself into Hannah's arms constructed of darkness.

They went on like this every day, her constantly reaching toward this perfection that, although he did not mind, Charlie did not desire at all. All day long, Hannah twisting and curving, until, at last, night would hit. And every night she'd have the same realization, well, he loved her just the way she was.

At sunset she felt truly perfect. When his warmth reached and wrapped around her but his seemingly judgmental light disappeared, she managed to feel just perfect.

They kissed, and it wasn't until the moment of connection ended, and Hannah started growing shorter again at sunrise, that the desire returned. Entirely the wrong desire. Rather than desire one another all she could desire was herself, in a selfish obsession with perfection.

# We feel angry when others go unscathed

Dedicated to Natasha Quattro

You fantasize about them arriving, arriving and dropping to their knees. You're lost in it, absorbed in it. If it were a body of water, you'd be slipping into this dream of goings on. On their knees, staring up so deeply into your eyes, they'd bestow a bouquet of flowers upon you, extending them upward.

Only, rather than grasp the sweet scented things, you'd twine your fingers through their hand and somewhere between gingerly and quite roughly you'd pull them to their feet. You smile at the thought of it, perhaps smiling to have hands together again perhaps smiling to feel, if only for a moment, in control.

So there they'd stand, wide eyes, searching yours. And they'd murmur "I'm here to ask you for a second chance."

Your pollen laden heart skips a beat.

You'd lean in, close, close to their ear so that they'd get a rich whiff of your scent. You'd just barely let your surfaces touch. A taste again of what they'd given up. And you would prepare to murmur back.

But first soft kisses along their windswept jawline, cold on your sun-heated lips. The kisses would progress and take you along a path straight to their lips. And there you'd be. You'd kiss them again.

Your pollen laden heart skips a beat.

He used to sweep the pollen away when he blew past.

The kiss would feel so entirely the same. Infinitely different, but the flavor and the feel is eternal. So you would get heady for a moment and probably feel that love again for a moment. It would be there, in reach, buried in the kiss.

But this would not be the sweet part. The sweet part is when you pull away and part your lips, begin, "Of course," pause.

And then you'd throw that bouquet crashing down to the ground. You'd smile as the petals splinter, a hopeless mess, over the dirt. Like your petals had. He'd have to see it then and think of what you'd been through.

You'd continue, "not." Of course not! No second chances! You'd turn on your heel and over your shoulder call back, "should've thought of this before" and behind you you would slam the door.

What a pretty fantasy.

Except that this will never happen to Hannah. No matter how many times she dreams it or how deeply she craves it. Charlie will never come a-knocking at her petal doors.

No, that windy wonder left determined. Determined to never think of her, the way she felt or feels. He was expelling Hannah from his life and ready to breeze by new flower faces. Never looking back. Never begging the resurrection of what they had.

She wants the satisfaction. She wants the redemption. Because Hannah has been living in a world of hurt, only now she's certain that the hurt is just anger.

Blazing red every time she spots another rose pressing lips to the sky, she is angry. It seems impossible that she was the one abandoned, when all along she'd thought she knew her place. Place on his pedestal of love. And yet persistently is the image of him walking away. She wants the opportunity to proclaim it, though, establish that she doesn't need him. Tell him that she doesn't want him either. Or better yet that despite his wanting her she does not want him, not an inkling of want.

She wants to slam the door in his face.

And so immersed in this fantasy, picturing the broken, cracked look on his face, she feels the same expression emerge on her own. Stem wracked by sobs, she's swaying in the air even without Charlie. Dew drop tears spilling. Petals cringing inward. Yes! She's angry! Bright red!

But her white rose petals say otherwise.

If he was at her door, she'd usher him in. If he begged forgiveness she'd already have offered. That kiss would never end, never let him out of her arms again.

Because, in fact, if she so much as saw his face it wouldn't be Charlie begging for a second chance. It would be Hannah, down on flower knees, so ready to plead.

Don't tell her, though. She doesn't know this yet. She's certain she's angry. So keep that bit to yourself.

# We take what we can get when there isn't much for getting

Dedicated to Jenna Royal

You need their approval the most. It hardly makes sense. Because they've rarely got it to offer.

But you need it, need to hear them say that you do all right. You'd think that you'd go for the easy catch. All the others who dip and swoon at every opportunity, easily impressed or perhaps just appreciative. But you need that hard to get, you need that unattainable. You're always up for a challenge.

You don't understand your actions.

This could be so easy, so easy to walk away from the pain. You chase things, though; it's the best way you know how to get what you want. The same way you chase the sun to get your favorite taste and the same way your roots extend so quickly in pursuit of what you need, you chase Charlie. Follow his every move.

That's your best shot at tender words. And God do you need tender words, now more than ever. Because for a four leaf clover you've been unlucky. You keep getting knocked down.

And funny that the one knocking you down is the one you love, the one you persist after. That's what love does right? Eliminates the pain?

Because he can drown her over and over and over and Hannah will still only see love eyes. Twinkling in the nighttime. She doesn't realize it's just the reflection of stars on his surface.

Hannah grew up right next to Charlie, the river bed next door. From the moment she saw him she predicted the love. Could see it coming a tide away.

What she did not foresee was the hate.

Perhaps it was his superiority, constant need for power, after all he was awfully more wide than Hannah, but whatever it was he was always happy to hurt her. He masked it with love, immense love at first.

"Your leaves are so green," were his first words to her, and she offered back a shy smile. It filled her up; she loved his approval. And somehow that rapidly turned into a she loved HIM.

But once he had her immersed, that was when the pummeling started. Couldn't let her get too comfortable. It was all out of love. Didn't want to lose her.

So he drowned her with cruelty.

Subtle cruelty, the kind that seeps and sneaks below the ground and takes root, holds a plant down. With little suggestions. Perhaps she'd be more beautiful if she reached a bit higher toward the sun. Like this? No, she was not quite beautiful enough like this. And don't say that Hannah! I don't appreciate your opinion, he came to say. Don't want to hear it anymore.

You're so needy, he'd tell her. But who could blame her for the need? She was barely gasping for air. Until finally he did her in. And she settled. Hannah accepted that sweet words were not for her and that she indeed was too pale a green, with too short a stem, and too sad a smile. He resented her more when she settled into the despair, but he basked in her having surrendered herself entirely. Slipped below his surface. Somehow desperate for his love when there was clearly no love to offer.

Maybe Charlie hadn't noticed.

Maybe he was unaware how deeply she'd come to rely, and how deep below the water he'd pushed her.

Maybe he didn't know clovers were designed for drowning.

Eventually he couldn't stand her sadness anymore, so he retreated back to the riverbed.

A clover cough, a choking. Hannah couldn't breathe. She laid there on the shore all broken up. She really was pale then, really was short of stem, and really, truly was sad. At least, she believed it was so.

You find yourself gasping for breath.

How did you get here? You'll ask yourself in retrospect. When in reality, it's quite obvious. You were so desperate for love words that you accepted them even when paired with hate. But perhaps hate carries more weight than love. You know how you got here, washed up in self-hate. Someone served it up to you on a silver plate, and with teeth hungry for any regard, you ate.

# We feel jealous when there's nothing for holding onto

Dedicated to Diane Clark

You're the jealous type. You think most people are. At least a little jealous. Only, you aren't just average. You feel it like a sickness. An infection, coursing through you and it's so painful it causes you to do things you otherwise would never even think of.

It's on your mind all the time. Who are they with? Why do they stare that way? Why do those words sound the same said to me as to anyone else?

Selfishly, you want someone just for you. Someone who's looking for somewhere to belong. You searched and searched, until you stumbled upon Hannah.

Hannah with her show stopping colors. You'd never seen light like her before. She was absolutely perfect for you.

Every shade embodied in her curving body, she was, infinitely, interesting. You could stare at her for days.

And she kept up silly conversations. The kind that sweep around bends. But you were sure there was something more to her at the end. So she had the beauty, the mystery, and the colorful smile. You figured you might chase this rainbow for a while.

Charlie too had his appeals. He was, infinitely, interested. Always surrounding things. He embraced them and encircled them and slipped into all the spaces between. Made them feel special. Always asking misty questions, always looking for discovery.

Hannah thought he looked interesting down below. Because at first he admired her from afar. Way down just above the ground, he smiled up at her. With such good intentions he sparked conversation with her. And soon they were talking all day.

She whispered to him the location of her pot of gold. He weaved through trees and streams, a fog filling the forest.

Charlie swept the floor until he found her. And he, seemingly greedily but truly out of fear of losing her, swept up every sparkling nugget.

Hannah was a bit perplexed, a bit offended. She had not expected so much so soon. But he felt cool and refreshing at her edges, caressing and distorting her light, creating light shows out of their kisses.

She was cautious.

All he intended was to love. But he had this tendency to doubt others. To doubt their commitment and even their love. It came off as obsessive, abrasive. Jealous.

Hannah was not one for jealousy. She just personally could not relate. Then again, she shined so bright that no one ever even considered leaving her. So it wasn't really fair in that way. He was misunderstood. He never figured out how else to feel. How to hold on tightly without a tendency for choking.

Still, despite such excuses, she couldn't stand it. All the questions, all the stares, the constant glances and insecurities. Asking about clouds, reflective lakes, anything that could compete. It made her sad at first, sad that he couldn't see her love. But sad could not last, and soon she was annoyed.

As Hannah began to pull away, further up into the sky, Charlie panicked. He rushed upward, a massive entity headed for the heavens. And in his misty jealous haze he surrounded her, blocked out the world.

But really he was blocking out Hannah. Because he could not even stand the idea of another so much as looking at her. He kissed every surface of her and begged her to understand. She was just too beautiful.

Resorting to bad behavior in desperation, he was suffocating her. And what Charlie did not foresee was that he'd begun to block out the light.

"How can I love you?"

Only she meant it literally, because how could she even go on without a light source? She was fading in his arms.

Charlie sobbed, a torrential downpour from his misty abyss. He could not say exactly why he was so certain she could not stay loyal. Because she was too beautiful? Too fun? Too easy to be with? Altogether too perfect. And he needed her, needed her. To be his and his alone. Guarded, guarding. He couldn't let go. Gripping, gripping, grappling for her presence. He called this desperation. And it was voiced in his watery sobs.

Until there was nothing left at all.

Only a shadow where the rainbow had been.

You may think that your jealousy speaks admiration, that it will enlighten someone to just how much you care about them. Otherwise you wouldn't behave in such a way. And it seems the safest, behaving jealously, if you want to keep your grip on all that you love. You may not realize, though, the tendency for your jealousy to jeopardize. Not until it's strangled your love dry.

# We can compromise until we're at the end of the line

Dedicated to Darlene Kanzler

When you want something different, you need something different. You'd like to say that all you want is them. But that's not for you. You need so much more.

You crave the whole wide world. And they're ready to settle down. You crave exploration. All they want to explore is you.

When you hear it it makes you smile a while. Such commitment and love. And then you remember how you really feel. Certainly not that way. And it makes you ill, darken a bit. It would be different if they wanted the same things. Craved also to soar. If you could claim as much in common as you have in disparity now, then perhaps your love could flourish.

They want to watch your love grow from the ground, though, and you need more. Aren't meant for rooting down.

If only it was easy. Easy for either of you to say the words. "We simply have different desires. It's not you. It's not me. It's we."

But no one has the guts to say it. Not when you're so in love. Because you're in denial and the mere thought of existing without them, even with the opportunity to pursue all that you want, it makes you sick too.

Hannah, a light wave accelerating toward Charlie, but also back toward the sky, felt this constant combination of pains. Stinging when she imagined light without him, stinging when she imagined going dark in his shadow. Charlie was, after all, a tremendous canopy; his problem was that he was content there on the ground.

She imagined bringing him with her, gathering up his yellowing leaves and turning them green again in the light. For a moment it was tremendous. Their light life together, pursuing together all that she dreamed of. And then reality would strike again and remind her that he had no interest in coming with her. Only loving her. Loving her, and convincing her to stay put with him there on the forest floor.

She needed more.

So it became a battle between love and life. Did she value more what she did or who she did it with? Having Charlie's arms around her or extending her own to the sky? The questions were beginning to strangle her. Because how could she decide? In her youth, having just parted from the sun, she saw herself as half of a whole and, once she'd met Charlie, felt as if she'd be broken were they to part.

And maybe there was someone else out there? Someone who could see and agree in her light? But she couldn't bear the thought. Not as she wove patterns through his leaves. Felt the kisses which simultaneously hurt. Hurt because they felt numbered. Numbered because freedom was awash in her mind.

Blinded by her own desire light.

Desire for Charlie or desire to live free?

It's hard to say when she decided precisely. Or if she ever chose at all, or if she simply passively remained wherever her love lived. But years later Hannah found herself a shadow. Dim compared to the ambitious, desirous light she'd been. It felt a bit like waking up. And suddenly she was staring up at the leaves which had decided her fate, fate to reach only across the ground, illuminating blades of grass and always his leaves. When obviously she'd been meant for the sky. Meant for more. Love means sacrifice. And she'd gone and sacrificed herself. Sacrificed a light life. Regret? No, never regret while still bundled in his branchy arms. Yet there were the tears flowing.

# We live in memories because we're lost in the now

Dedicated to Kelsea Critin

The things that remind you, well, every little thing reminds you. You wonder if your mind is disordered or diseased. Because it simply doesn't make sense, that every scent on a breeze takes you back to one of your moments. Every sound that waivers past reminds you of some setting, some words, murmured quietly or cried out in ecstasy. Each sight looks like something which looks like them, or merely contains the color of their eyes, or even vaguely resembles some shape, the shapes etched into their skin, the shape of their hug, the shape of their kiss.

You can't escape it.

You feel strange sometimes, so obviously living in the present but somehow simultaneously living always in the past. Shouldn't you be here, now? Except you are, you just turn every corner expecting to see someone from the past. You open your eyes every morning and emerge from a dream written in memories. Expecting to wake up in their arms. Your own bed of river stones reminds you of them. Their scent is stuck there. The indent of their shape still appears to be there, in that shallow spot amidst the rocks.

It doesn't make sense.

You've explained it to other water worn rocks, and they never understand. No, they always beg the question, how is it even possible? How can everything bring on a memory?

Charlie eventually realized, though, that the problem was not the sights and sounds and smells around him, not the currents and bubbling and the scent of the rain as it pitter pattered. It was not the sensations that were the issue; it was the fact that the only thing always on his mind was Hannah.

And all of these other things entered, and he processed them, but he processed them through Hannah stained film or a Hannah shaped filter. Everything could be tied to her in some way, and so everything was. In this fatal thought flaw Charlie managed to always relive pain. Because although the memories he selected were sweet there was always the underlying current, like the current washing over him, so that the sweet could only be bitter. He looked up at the sun and saw her algae eyes. Only, remembering the eyes meant remembering the disgusted look in them as she rushed away, rushed onto the closest stream that would carry her far away.

Everything inspired memory and every memory brought on ache. So he was always stone heart aching.

This is the world he chooses to live in. A world laced with persistent pain. Because Charlie lives in memories of Hannah. Because Charlie loves Hannah so.

But her algae eyes are only a memory now.

You taste the memories and they taste so sweet. You cling to them, like some life line, only your rope was severed long ago. And you're left drifting in your river of sorrow, always tugging in hopes of being pulled aboard the love dock.

But the dock's splintered and sank. So the closest thing you've got to life is memories.

# We feel guarded until no one's interested

Dedicated to Nicole Craft

What do you do when you're in love with someone who lives always behind closed doors? You ask them how they're feeling, they say "fine". You ask them what they're thinking, they say "nothing". You ask them to open up, they say "all right". You ask them what they're doing, and without you they're getting high. Which drugs? They say opiates, no need to specify. Why do you want to go numb? Not sure, why?

These are your conversations, as you press an awaiting ear against the blackened rock. She's in there somewhere and you think you're close.

But what do you do next? What do you do when you're desperately in love with someone who only allows you to exist on the surface?

You've told yourself you ought to walk away, that someone so secretive isn't worth your time. You crave an open book, someone who you can relate to.

The issue is, a part of you knows her. A part of you delved momentarily, from the edge of the volcano, deep into her inferno. And you fell in love with the heat there.

But you loved her even before that. Hannah was an enigmatic, bubbling surface. She was awash with reds and brilliant golds. Always expelling heat, pleasant hints of who she really was. Once you'd felt her there was no going back.

She was so beautiful even from afar. Molten magma, she flowed and danced seductively like she had liquid hips and fire instead of lips. When you kissed her it hardly seemed to matter that she had yet to murmur a serious word.

Because Charlie wasn't so certain that seriousness was necessary anyhow. Couldn't a relationship thrive on the surface, his breezy currents always swimming in this heat? Plenty of couples lived on the surface like this, leaving the personal just that, to each his or her own.

But from time to time he wondered if she needed it, needed windy conversation. As he brushed past he always tried. And he opened up, spilled his deepest insecurities, the fear that he'd lose control, cause such gusts that he hurt those around him or that he might simply sputter into a gentle breeze, and that in this she might stop loving him. She nodded and bubbled reassuring words.

But nothing else.

She did not usher him below the surface.

When you want to know someone so desperately, when you're trying and trying yet you remain so far apart. What more can you say, do? They already said that they love you. And so why do you at times feel that they are a stranger? Is it something you did wrong?

The way that Hannah refused to trust Charlie tore him apart, left him laden with pockets of air. From time to time he lashed, ripping across her surface. Just tell me, just talk to me! He'd cry. And she retreated deeper into her heat.

Not a word, not a moment of connection.

What do you do when someone you love so dearly is so very close, and yet 90% of them feels infinitely far away? And no matter how far you trek, how much you pry, they just don't trust you and can't admit why. He wished she was active, that in a burst she might just spill over. Then he would see every drop of hot lava, know every part of Hannah.

She took him infinitely for granted. What more could he do? After one final try, he warned her. If you don't show me your true colors I'll have no choice but to leave.

There's nothing to show, she insisted, but her pained expression revealed otherwise.

And then Charlie was gone, frustrated and lost on some new current, some current that would take him far away from Hannah.

She remembered all his words, his secrets. There was a sick pride in that he knew none of hers. She retained her dignity in that she could almost insist that she'd been alone. Who knows Hannah? Well, no one, not even her true love.

She did not recognize how sad this was until he was gone. And suddenly her lava felt so hot that it became cold. He loved me, and I couldn't meet him halfway, she thought, bubbling with a newfound pain.

He'd always been there, so for a while she played herself and presumed he'd be back. Charlie had made a promise though. The air was still.

And at last in a pulsing sob she burst, or more so overflowed in what could only be described as the most pathetic eruption. Lava coursed over her tough exterior, and finally she was exposed, only for the first time no one was listening. Hannah hardened, black and cold, even more impenetrable than ever before. What do you do when you're in love with someone always tugging at the handles of your doors? The hinges are too fragile, you simply couldn't let them in. You tell them how you're feeling, you're fine. You tell them what you're thinking, you think of nothing. And there's an entire inferno of secrets somewhere below. But as far as you're concerned, in order to love they don't really need to know.

# We call it love because we don't know its name

Dedicated to Diane Clark

You are the most on again off again, the most volatile, polar opposites; like magnets, you perpetually repel and attract. So you live in a constant state of disarray, on a roller coaster of love and pain, hope and hate. Can we make it work this time? Let's just talk, we'll facilitate a conversation, you say through misty mouths. Only, the words are dissipating as soon as they slip through your lips.

You live in love and hate.

And it pains you. But you won't let it hurt you. Nothing phases you, either of you. Because for water you're both a lot more like ice in the sky.

On again off again.

Hannah and Charlie rose to the sky in claims that they loved each other. They were attracted together, tiny droplets of vapor accumulating together until they'd formed rounded and soft poofy white clouds. These were love clouds, and they were pretty to look at for a while.

On again.

And then something as simple as a breeze, or one additional droplet of water, and suddenly the pair of clouds darkened, darkened into a blackness that wrote the word hate across the sky.

Most clouds experienced storms. None could remain wispy or cumulus forever. But the frequency with which Hannah and Charlie billowed into blackness, and the intensity with which they raged, well, it was devastating.

And not just to the pair.

Though they were too selfish to see the damage which they caused, it was immense. Thunder booming and deafening all that surrounded them and from time to time a crack of lightning on one poor passerby. They were damaging physically, but also setting a horrific example.

The water droplets below feared evaporating, ever rising to the sky, worried about a fate as love sickening as Hannah and Charlie's.

Because what was a love when so twisted and wrought with hate? They called it passion, said they were passionate clouds. But the rumbling in the sky often crossed the fine line between passion and anger. Love and hate.

The reflection of lightning across a calm pond in the sky left it quaking with fear. Never would this body of water seek out love, because look at the pain it garners.

Only, Hannah and Charlie did not see it as pain. They'd been through this cycle so many times that hate became natural, started to feel right. And they regretted it when one ended up shriveled and damaged, wilted and water free, voice hoarse from roaring and all light drained from zipping lightning. But both were too proud ever to apologize.

And too proud to change their ways.

Every time they started fresh they were certain things would be different. They cuddled close like cotton balls and the water below looked on in awe. Had they not just crashed together in stormy rage? And here Hannah and Charlie were whispering love words on soft winds as they rolled by.

Off again.

They're crashing and burning and this time they say that they're better off leaving the skies blue, giving up even on trying. And the world below sighs relief. Because although they'd like to see love, love seems impossible for two clouds so twisted and damaged. Incapable of real love, only this joke of it that's a mask for hate.

On again off again.

And there's a forest burned down from a spark in the lightning and a flood elsewhere, countless plants torn to pieces and the ground is a mess of mud. They don't see this damage, only glare resentfully at one another and proclaim that this is the last time.

Passion, though, is a tricky thing.

Because in the glare and the murmuring of forgiveness it feels like love to them. The hate bred emotions they couldn't comprehend, so they twisted them like a puzzle until it read something they could understand. They kissed again, accumulating just above the ground. Interlocked watery fingers. Hadn't there been something here before? For so long Hannah had belonged to Charlie. And Charlie to Hannah. They knew nothing else.

So they called it love again and settled into the sky. The water below, at some point, had disappeared, all the ponds and rivers simply gone dry.

# We feel guilty when there's nothing to be done

Dedicated to Nicole Craft

You're on the verge of being disgusted with yourself, on the verge of despising this half of a whole you've become. Because in reality you are not nearly close to half, despite the fact that you know just how awful it is to be on the other side, to be the one always in wanting, always loving more. You know how degrading that is, how helpless you feel.

You've been there before.

Charlie left you in that dark place once before.

And here you are now, with this other hopeless, lovesick star, and you aren't even close to half. He makes up for the gap, though. You simply can't muster the emotion to love so much.

You loved much more once before.

Are you ashamed? Perhaps not ashamed, but you're guilty. You ask yourself if it wouldn't be better to just let them go altogether. Then they'd have a shot at finding their true other half. Not this 40-60 nonsense. 30-70 the more you think about it.

It isn't that this star doesn't shine bright enough, or that his fiery core doesn't burn hot enough. In fact, you just about think he's perfect. Any other planet would be lucky to have him, you're sure.

So why can't Hannah embrace him? That isn't the issue at hand, though. The issue here begs the question, how do you eliminate this eminent guilt? This desire to be equal in an inherently disparate situation?

Thus far Hannah had found that every star and planet relationship left one member less loved. In the past, she'd been certain it was worse being the romantic, the desirer, the one always chasing. But suddenly, as desiree, she wasn't so sure.

Because it made her sick when he looked at her with those hopeful starlight eyes. And when he said I love you and she could not quite respond. She felt like a tyrant in the world of their love. A measly planet leaving such a bright star in a pool of light desperation.

He only shined brighter and brighter.

She tried to reflect the love light back, but maybe it just wasn't in Hannah's nature. No, that was an excuse. She had it in her, just not for his taking. Her greatest love had been consumed and what was left of it put on reservation for one star and one star alone. Charlie.

So it was unfair to play this game, to be the one in power despite the fact that she did not crave it. Hannah, with sagging shoulders and a sigh, wondered why this power even came into play. Why relationships entailed roles of intensity that are bound to harm those involved.

So what's worse? Hurting or being hurt? It seems a silly question, but the guilt and desire for change so consumed her that she was cracking on the inside, a splintered planet releasing space dust into the sky.

She remembered just how it felt on the other side. Maybe it was empathy that had her so broken up.

She remembered the insecurity, always probing with love-wrought eyes for the pupil-contact that never reassured her. Always reaching out to touch his light in hopes he might reach as far back toward her. Nights of crying and days of hoping, but never quite feeling equal. Charlie was always just out of reach, always a little too distant, always a little less interested.

And now she was bestowing this on someone else? She was cruel, she was everything that she'd resented in Charlie.

But she remembered that too.

The way you can't really resent someone, not when you love them so much. This star, though probably awash with negative feelings, could not feel any toward her specifically. She saw it in his starlight eyes. In the way he embraced her. Yes, he was always hoping, hoping she was his other half, but never giving up on fulfilling that whole regardless of her participation.

How could she be doing this to another?

The star asked her what was wrong, because he was just that kind of guy. Unconditional love, always seeing when something went awry. She almost resented the way that he cared for her.

"I can't feel the way that you do."

And all he said was, "As long as I'm with you I really don't mind."

# We feel determined despite the walls between us

Dedicated to Calvin Borchers

You live now through panes of glass, extending frothy fingers toward her. Always reaching, always thinking you're getting closer. But you're suspended and really you aren't going anywhere.

This is incapacitated. This is when the world screws you over and there is literally nothing to be done. It isn't a matter of screwing up, not anything you did, not anything they did. The ice is prickling up your spine. Seeing her, this close, it's taunting, tingling; it hurts.

For a moment, suspended, because you have infinite moments to ponder, you're pondering. And you're thinking, well, it would almost be better if we'd done something wrong, if, in fact, the love was truly gone. But it's right there and it's just out of reach. You're frustrated.

You're frustrated in that you can see the love, can almost touch it, almost taste it. You remember that it tastes salty. And that memory, this close to being your reality, makes you angry.

Charlie's foamy anger had nowhere to go, though, simply remained suspended with him in the ice. He could feel his edges rippling. So ready to come crashing down. But this ice prison had him shaped in the loveless beginnings of a wave, rather than the foamy crashing rich with love bubbles bursting, rising up to the surface of Hannah's sea skin just meters away. Ice droplets reaching, extending, reaching. So close. But desperately far.

You never really considered that love could hurt this way. You've felt the pain of betrayal or loss of love, resentment and pure sadness when there's something better, when something goes wrong. But this? This mere distance? It's new to you.

A whole new pain, one that so many have felt before you but that feels entirely yours. It belongs to you and you alone here, right now, when you're reaching for her and you aren't sure that you'll ever get there.

When barriers divide Hannah and Charlie, when their love is strangled from air by the hands of distance, mere distance and nothing more, it feels so unnecessarily hopeless.

Because they're so close, but the world won't bring them together. That cold iciness that froze Charlie mid-motion was not backing off. And though Hannah lapped at his frigid edges there was really no hope for connection.

That deep frustration cracking him at his base, but never enough to splinter him, ice encased, back into her arms. When you are incapacitated, inches away but worlds apart, and it feels like you're staring through a pane of glass, and every time a tear drop emerges it freezes just inches from your face, always in front of you to remind you, to remind you of what could be a minuscule distance, but which ends up leaving you an eternity apart.

Tear drops pour, like a free for all. Charlie's crying not for his inability to love her but for the desperation. He's just this close, foamy fingertips reaching, but never reaching far enough. Only it's not the kind of thing where if he just tried harder, reached farther; they're doomed to this frozenness. This frozen fate. Always waiting. Never changing, because no matter what they say or do the ice won't crack, won't grow porous.

When the world around you simply will not allow you to love. Everything is there, every emotion, every trace of love. Only isolated, encased in ice. You can't taste it, can't touch it. Just out of reach.

# We feel love with contact until contact defines our love

Dedicated to Lizzie Garcia

Touch is like medicine for you. You were once averse to it, shy. It grew on you, though, the more you were exposed. First something to avoid, then something you didn't mind, and then something you craved, until finally it was something that you needed.

Touch became like a cold pack on a burn, pressure on a bleed, novacaine against pain, and a mind boggling fog when things got really excruciating. You hate to admit it, but touch means a lot to you. And touch is a crucial part of a relationship. You'd like to say it would be the same had you lost the inability to physically connect, if all you had left were the wind whispers and the ability to see her jostling about, tossing around your flames. But you know that, in reality, it would be near impossible to live without the feel of her.

Hannah felt the same, though she figured she ought to not let on. The fiery passion that she rushed against, though, it felt like he was bringing her to life. Touching fire is like no other sensation, the deepest heat and greatest intensity. She loved the way he could burn her up.

It was a bit of an unspoken thing between them, this craving for touch. Neither of them had ever recognized its value until they'd laid flaming fingertips and cool breezy lips on one another. Now that they had, though, desire consumed them upon looking at each other.

And still their conversations were cool and of respectable things and they didn't dare mention their respective experiences of being consumed by such a need. She could see it in his white light eyes, though.

And he saw it in the way she curved on the breeze.

It was a dance: who can resist the longest? Play it off like they aren't interested? Barely caress but never hold, lips hardly press but nothing more bold?

This dimension of things was a whole new dynamic. Because Hannah and Charlie had loved each other so deeply for such a long time. She loved his warmth, rather than his heat, and his crackling conversation. And he loved the way she could whistle and weave through the sky.

Yet suddenly they wanted more, wanted always to be intertwined. And one evening Hannah begged herself the question, can you touch too much? Because in all the sweet kissing something else had gone missing.

And suddenly there wasn't much to say anymore. Wasn't much to look at in wonder. No more love words, no more late night lullabies.

The substance was gone and, less like a craving, touch became the only thing. It was all they had left. How had it happened? When had Hannah slipped through his fire fingers? When had Charlie disappeared within the flames?

Hannah grew weaker with each passing sunrise, from a gust to a light breeze until finally she could hardly even rustle leaves. And in her absence Charlie was growing dimmer. Out of nowhere, it stopped feeling like much of anything at all.

They were strangers groping at empty surfaces, running elemental hands over each other in search of the lovers that once were there. And all that was left was the heat.

They say that things go wrong when the passion's gone, but what about when passion is all that remains? When you don't know the person who holds you? Hannah faltered, slipping from the sky to the Earth, ashamed that all she knew how to do was kiss, and in that agony Charlie lost his flame.

# The Secret Garden

Dedicated to those who have hope

You've managed to flutter into a secret garden. Not sure how you got here, you're just beginning to absorb your surroundings. And they're breathtaking. Absolutely, and you're so pleased with your discovery.

When had you flown in? The funny thing about this place was that it hardly seemed secret. The gates were wide open, wrought iron black curling and twisting to spread wide. It was a clear window in, into the secret garden. Yet no others were here.

So it must be secret.

It makes little sense. Such a beautiful place would normally attract endless others. And here it is just for you, quiet except for the dripping of water and trickling of sunlight onto open wide flower petal mouths. Perhaps you just haven't found them yet. Perhaps the garden isn't so secret.

An idea overcomes you then. Maybe it isn't secret to you, with those wide open gates and welcoming, curling iron fingers, but maybe secret to all the other creatures out there. A secret garden designed just for your finding. Maybe they can't make out the edges, can't see the gates, all the others, not the way that you do. And it's because you had eyes that were searching.

Not searching out of some need. But you were open to it, open to finding new experience because your butterfly life had grown a bit mundane.

It was unclear to you then if the mundaneness was a product of your setting or those around you. Impossible to say.

This garden, though, seems like the change of pace that you need. Endless blooming flowers billow out from the ground extending toward you as if offering a taste. The grass is a green that seems abuzz with energy, electric, and from here the sky looks bluer than it ever did before. The water is more refreshing; the trees reach higher; the sun heats the air around you to that sweet spot, lemon drop temperature which makes your wings feel so light and alive. Every breeze carries you a bit further here and you think you've found where you belong.

It has a way of making you feel special.

Only, you find yourself turning every corner in anticipation of another. As you weave through wind currents, you over and over think you hear the soft murmur of others' wings. And soon enough it's obvious that even in the comfort of solitude you're craving the presence of another. This would be perfect, you're thinking, if you had the opportunity to share it with someone else.

Your secret garden.

You aren't sure you want to claim it all for your own. Ready to let someone in, maybe a secret for two.

Your flight pattern is becoming more frantic as you fly. And your breaths are gasping and your antennae prostrate in search. What can you find? You're in a secret garden after all.

You're certain, though, that there's got to be another out there who thinks like you do. Who would be able to discern the gate too. And you realize that anyone you might find in this secret garden would inherently be perfect for you. Because if here is where they belong and here is where you belong, then together you belong.

This place fits you so perfectly, every shape designed to fit your wings and curve along your spine. The air is your favorite flavor here. And the whole place it just makes you smile sigh because it's entrancing and leaves you feeling entranced in thought, in contented thought. You haven't thought this way in a while.

Anyone else so contented here could be contented with you, you decide. And anyone else who's wings fit precisely between the slots in the trees and who perch, weight distributed just so, on flower stems and petals could fit just so along your lips, you're sure. A kiss designed for the two of you, like this place, love designed for the two of you.

Whipping around a corner, you almost pass them by. Almost mistake them for another pretty flower. But you hear the soft, subtle sound of their exhale. Suddenly, the shape of their curving wings is so obvious and the spiraling of their antennae is the most beautiful spiraling you've ever seen.

"Wait!" they call after you. Because they've been waiting too.

And on the most gentle of breezes you cease the movement of your wings, allow the wind to carry you to their side. Your vision subsides, to a white glow, and you can't feel your legs beneath you. Like a temporary paralysis.

Because you're so surprised.

Because the secret garden had felt so right, like the ultimate belonging. And somehow, here, next to a love as lovely as you ever imagined, your perfect match, somehow, you feel even more right. Takes your breath away.

Regaining consciousness, you breathe in unison, and at each other you smile.

32886706R00099

Made in the USA
Charleston, SC
26 August 2014